VICIOUS VET

A COCKY HERO CLUB PRODUCTION

ASHLEY MUNOZ

Editor: C. Marie
Proofreading by: Cocky Hero Club and Ashley Munoz
Cover Design: NetHook Line and Design
Formatted by: Ashley Munoz

Vicious Vet is a standalone story inspired by Vi Keeland and Penelope Ward's Cocky Bastard. It's published as part of the Cocky Hero Club world, a series of original works, written by various authors, and inspired by Keeland and Ward's *New York Times* bestselling series.

✻ Created with Vellum

1

KELLY

"Hey, this is Aubrey. Leave a message after the beep and I'll get back to you."

I winced, hopping on one leg as I shoved my foot into one of my new-to-me Mandolina pumps. This was the third round of phone tag my boss Aubrey and I had played over the past two weeks. Normally she wasn't this evasive or unavailable. I hadn't heard of anything changing in her schedule, and since I was getting regular emails, I at least knew she was okay.

But, damn, I needed to actually have a conversation with the woman, because I was out of my depth.

The previous week, I'd started as the new manager of operations at the Park Street Animal Shelter. It wasn't a match made in heaven or anything, more like a patch job on a ripped pair of jeans, or the superglue keeping a pair of heels together just so someone could finish out the workday.

That was me, patch-job Kelly. There to cover and help in any way I could. Reliable, dependable, and *utterly pathetic.*

"Hey Aubrey, it's me again, Kelly...look, I need to talk to you about this email I received from Julie. She said something about a camera crew arriving and the new vet being interviewed. I don't know what any of that means, so something must have been miscommunicated. Please call me back." I pressed the red end button and straightened.

I needed to review Julie's email again, because nothing was clear, and I was completely confused. I'd been on payroll for a total of six business days, and so far, nothing—and I do mean nothing—had gone smoothly.

First, I nearly died from allergies just touring the facility. I would have turned the job down then, but Aubrey begged me to reconsider. I have the schooling under my belt for running and managing the shelter, regardless of the fact that my first job out of college was as a personal assistant. Sure, that wasn't exactly in the plans; no one puts personal assistant down as their dream job. Mine had just happened to burst into flames my freshman year of college, so after graduation I saw that a local law firm was in need of an assistant for a new lawyer who had just started, and I applied. Fast forward three years and here I was, taking a job I had no idea how to actually do, just to avoid the unemployment line.

I grabbed my purse, my jacket, and frantically searched for my phone, belatedly realizing it was still in my hand.

"Shit, I'm so late," I huffed to absolutely no one, turning my wrist to catch the time. With not a spare second to check my makeup or hair, I shoved out of my front door and turned to lock it before bolting down the hall. Thankfully Jones, my neighbor, wasn't around to "shoot the breeze", as he so affectionally referred to what he liked to do from time to time, clogging up the elevator with creepy vibes and awkward compliments.

Rushing outside and toward the bus, I finally let out an exhalation as I situated myself on the uncomfortable cluster of bucket seats. To pass the time during the ten-minute commute, I pulled my phone out and opened the email from Julia, hoping to glean some new understanding from it.

It read exactly the same as it had the first time.

Ms. Thomas,

I received an email from Aubrey letting me know that the new veterinarian will be coming in tomorrow. She said a news crew will be accompanying him. She also said you might want to dress nice and be ready to answer some questions about fundraising and donations for the shelter.

See you bright and early,

Julie

I wrinkled my eyebrows in confusion. Why on earth would a news crew be coming in with the vet? Furthermore, why on earth would our animal shelter need a full-time vet? I mean, I suppose those big box pet stores had vet clinics and pet grooming inside, and this wouldn't really be any different. Maybe the camera crew was just coincidentally timed and had nothing at all to do with the arrival of the vet. That was probably it. Still, it would have been nice to hear directly from Aubrey. She'd moved closer to LA to be with her husband, Chance, and since the entire firm I used to work for had up and left, I was just left here to figure things out.

It was fine. Everything would be fine. I was going on day seven, my allergy medication was finally working, and I had finally nailed the morning commute from my building. The bus pulled up to the curb, and my surrounding bus-mates all stood, shuffling in order to exit. As soon as I was free, I bolted out toward the only coffee spot on this end of town, praying to everything holy that I wouldn't trip in my shoes. They might have been discounted, but they'd still cost upwards of two hundred dollars.

Pushing in through the glass door of the local coffee shop, I exhaled as I approached the counter.

"Hi there. Large Americano with cream, please." I smiled briefly, right as my phone rang. I let out a disappointed sigh as I answered it. "Hey, sis."

"Hey, don't sound so excited," Selah droned while the sound of kids yelling in the background reverberated in my ear.

I eyed the barista as she filled the cup of the person in front of me. "Sorry, I was expecting Aubrey to call."

"Still playing phone tag, huh?"

I let out another heavy sigh as someone bumped into my shoulder. "Yeah, things are crazy right now."

"Are you still good for dinner tonight?" she asked, raising her voice above the chaotic hollering in the background. I resisted the urge to pull the phone away from my ear.

"I'm not sure. I know I've canceled three times, but I just started this job."

"I know, but Jonathan keeps asking about you, and I hate putting him off because it seems like you're trying to ditch when I know that's not true. You would really like him," she insisted, and I could feel my heart wilt. My sister had been trying to set me up with different suitors for over a year and had just recently found out that her husband's best friend was interested in me. In her mind, it would be some kind of dream matchup if I dated—or had *something more* with—him.

"I know," I murmured, seeing my cup make its way to the counter. "Okay, look…I'll make it work."

"You will?" she screeched excitedly.

"Yeah. Six, right? I'll be there—gotta go, love you." I hung up and grabbed my coffee.

The white paper cup burned my fingers as I charged down the block toward the shelter. To make matters even more exciting, it started to rain.

"Come on," I moaned, ducking my head to protect my makeup. I rushed around the corner and in through the double glass doors, tightening my grip on the scalding cup, defiant until the end. I would not lose face and drop my coffee in front of my employees.

Again.

I wasn't used to the coffee shop I now frequented. The Starbucks near my old job never needed to provide a sleeve for the cup because the coffee was always the perfect temperature. Now, the Coffee Hut on First didn't know how *not* to scald their customers' tongues and obliterate their taste buds. My first day on the job, I had dropped the cup when I was halfway through the double doors, and everyone had taken notice. I do mean everyone.

The fluorescent lights blinked at me, still malfunctioning even after Kip had come to fix them. My left eye twitched in response, as though the stress was still stuck there from the previous week's fiasco.

"Do you need any help, Ms. Thomas?" Patty—or was it Natalie?—asked, leaning over the reception desk, watching me carefully. Our morning volunteer, she'd witnessed my first coffee disaster and looked as though she expected it every day since.

I smiled at her, noticing her long blonde hair covering the desk, her crop top rising with her movement. I resisted the urge to roll my eyes and bark at her to grab a shirt that fit. I was cranky. I'd been nothing but cranky since I started, and I hated myself for it. Inhaling short breaths through my nose, I shuffled faster to my office down the laminate floors, replying, "No, I've got it. Thanks."

What was I saying? I didn't have it—not at all. I should have passed the coffee on to her, should have begged for a paper towel or something to act as a barrier between the cup and my poor digits. I pushed forward faster, turning and about to push my back into my office door as I heard Patty yell, "Oh yeah, I nearly forgot, someone's in—"

Her words were cut off as I leaned against the door and it swung right into someone on the other side.

The jolt sent my hand into my chest, where my hotter-than-the-bowels-of-hell coffee poured down my crisp white shirt. *Fuckity-FUCK.*

It was so hot I wanted to scream, but an awkward moan-slash-whimper escaped instead.

Patty wrinkled her nose as she leaned over to see me more clearly. "Your office. Someone is in your office…that's what I was trying to say."

I gave her a scathing look and turned away before I said something to match my sour mood. I tossed the empty cup into the wastebasket and began brushing the excess liquid off my shirt. Call me unprofessional, but I didn't rush to meet the eyeline of whoever was in my office, because I'd been meeting new team members for the past week and I was a bit dazed by how many new faces I'd shoved into my memory.

"You always make those kinds of sounds when you spill shit on yourself?" a harsh voice scoffed from behind the door.

I still did not feel ready to meet his stare because I had coffee on my breasts and because it was laundry day—or month, to be honest—so I was sporting a hot pink, lacy bra under my shirt. I needed a second to gather myself before dealing with whoever this tool was.

Staring down at my ruined top, I merely replied with, "What kind of sounds...like I'm dying? Because I'm pretty sure anyone in my position would make death sounds."

Another scoff slipped from the man's lips. "Hardly...it was more like you were getting properly fucked, actually."

What the hell?

I turned and quickly assessed this crass jerk. My judgment-heavy eyes traveled up a pair of dark slacks and a perfectly pressed white shirt paired with a sleek blue tie...until finally I was met with a familiar set of cobalt eyes.

Ones that had once destroyed me.

I took a step back on instinct, because when one realizes they're in a confined space with a dangerous animal, one backs the hell up.

"Greyson..." I stammered, my voice caught in my throat. I cleared it and tried again. "What are you doing here?"

"Miss me, Kat?" He emphasized the T on the end of my nickname, just like he used to, and smirked.

My name being Kelly Arabella Thomas made it way too easy for this prick to give me a stupid nickname, one I hadn't heard fall from his lips in four long years, one that shouldn't have made me feel the way it had the last time I'd heard it.

Cold, unforgiving resolve settled into my core as I met his stare.

"No, not even a little bit. What the hell are you doing here? We had a deal." I walked around my desk, ensuring there was some kind of barrier between us.

"I've got a press conference this morning, it would seem. I've been traveling out of the country for a few weeks, and I wanted to ensure we were properly introduced before we went on camera. As you mentioned our deal, I am sure you can understand why." Perfect full lips that only looked better now than they had four years earlier smiled at me.

My brain wasn't firing as well without the coffee, but I tried to grasp what little things I could. Scanning the contents of my desk, I shuffled a few papers, trying to gather my thoughts until it registered.

No.

That could only mean…

"You're the new on-call vet?"

He stalked closer, his blond hair disheveled and gorgeous, way more than it had been in the past, falling gracefully over his left eyebrow.

"Yep. Looks like we'll be working together, boss." He smiled so wide his dimples popped, causing an avalanche of worry to swim through me.

No, no. *No.*

This couldn't be happening.

Refusing to show any weakness, I squared my shoulders, causing my chest to push out. Greyson's eyes dipped, and I immediately wanted to cross my arms.

Hadn't he done enough? Hadn't he taken enough from me?

"Well, as I told Aubrey, now that I'm taking things over, there might be some shifting of positions on the payroll. So, don't get too comfortable." I smiled at him, like the evil wench I'd turned into after he ruined me.

His eyes flickered with something that looked like hurt for just a brief second, but then he was smiling again. "Oh Kat, that's the best part of all this."

Confusion riddled my features. I felt it and hated that I couldn't hide it. "What do you mean?"

That smirk stayed in place as he turned for the door. "You might want to put on something a little less revealing—the camera guys are already setting up."

Then he was gone out of my office and I was still fumbling for air, for words…for some explanation for what in the hell had just happened, because Aubrey hiring my worst enemy of all time surely wasn't actually real.

"Julie." I pressed the intercom button on my phone and waited, but nothing happened, so I pressed the button for my assistant again. "Julie!"

"Ms. Thomas?" Our front desk volunteer shoved my door open with a worried expression on her face.

"What?" I sat down, trying to hide the disaster that was my shirt.

"Um…someone keeps talking into the phone out front." Her blue eyes furrowed into bewildered little slits.

Dammit.

"Where is Julie?" I asked, curt and annoyed.

"Um, she's in the kitchen." Front desk girl smiled and stood taller, causing her shirt to rise. I blinked and stood, not wanting to exit the safety of my office now that I knew Greyson was walking around the shelter.

"Okay, can you please ask her to come here? And please let her know it's an emergency," I opened the desk and hoped there would be an extra shirt somewhere in the drawers. There were shirts with the shelter's name printed on them; I had seen them before, so it made sense that they might be somewhere in the office.

Front desk girl twirled and left the room as I searched but she ran back in a brief second later.

"There are camera guys here and they thought I was you— they're ready for you." Her eyes went wide, her eyebrows hitting her hairline as she took in my appearance.

Fuckity. Fuck.

"Cammy, I'm going to need you to give me your shirt." I held out my hand.

"My name is Payton." She inched closer, eyes wide, staring at my hand.

"Payton, hand it over." I moved my hand forward, feeling a surge of apprehension hit my stomach as I considered what a shitshow this was going to be.

"My shirt?" Her voice rose into a squeak.

"Yes, your shirt. I'll trade you. I know mine is wet, but I have to go on TV. It'll only be for a few minutes." I moved around the desk and started unbuttoning my top.

Payton's eyes narrowed in confusion as I began to strip.

"Hurry, please—I'm begging you. I am literally begging you to trade me. I have no shirt, I haven't found any extra shelter t-shirts in this office anywhere, and I am out of time," I pleaded, pulling my arms out of the shirt.

Finally, she kicked it into gear and pulled her top over her head. "Here, sorry…" She fumbled and grabbed for my wet blouse. I felt horrible, fucking horrible, but what options did I have? I pulled her cream chemise over my head, wishing somehow the material would cover more of my stomach than it did. It had a low scoop neck, cinched tight at the waist, and was cropped at the belly button. On a teenage girl, it was adorable. On me, an actual adult, it was nearly pornographic.

I pulled it down only to have the scoop dip, and then I pulled the neckline only to have the waist lift above my belly button. *Dear, sweet Jesus.*

Blanching, I found a mirror in the swinging cabinet door, which unfortunately was lacking any t-shirts. I checked my hair, applied some lip gloss, and took in a swell of breath.

I can do this. I am going to figure this out, and it will be fine.

I opened the door as Payton hung back, drowning in my soaked dress shirt. "You can hang out here until I'm done, and if Julie pops in, please let her know I am in need of a new shirt as soon as possible."

I strode out, head held high and confident. I ignored the fact that my cleavage was on display and my midriff was showing. To make matters infinitely worse, my belly button piercing was in, making it look like I'd actually planned this little getup, like I wanted my debut television appearance to be done half-naked.

My nerves were totally shot as my heels clicked along the floor, toward the entrance of the shelter. With their backs turned to me, four men wearing a variety of denim jackets and flannel stood, two with a camera, one with a boom stick, and the other with a microphone. Greyson stood amongst them, his head bent in to read some sheet of paper. I pressed my nails into my palms as firmly as I could and stalked confidently toward the group.

"Hey everyone, I'm Kelly. Where do you need me?"

They all turned around, so many sets of eyes raking over me, assessing what they were seeing. My assistant Julie was across the room, holding a folder to her chest, and her face paled as soon as she saw me. Greyson's eyes perused slowly, from my chest to my navel, taking his time, like he owned every inch of my skin.

I refused to feel embarrassed. I refused to be anything but professional as everyone awkwardly made room for me next to Greyson.

He was the reason I looked like a hooker. It was his fault. I resisted the urge to point my finger and yell it, like a third grader.

"Okay, Ms. Thomas, um…" One of the cameramen struggled to meet my eyes. "I will get you wired, if you want to come over here." His face flushed, and I noticed a wedding ring on his finger, hating the shame that swam through me. *His wife probably hates my guts right now, or would if she were here.*

"Yeah, okay, thanks," I mumbled, walking closer. Greyson's presence was overbearing, sweltering, completely insufferable. He stood shoulder to shoulder with me, but because I was smaller, he practically towered over me.

"Okay, here you go." The camera guy fed a black wire up near my neck and carefully tucked it under my shirt through the back. Greyson's gaze tracked the movement, and I wouldn't have cared at all if not for the fact that his eyebrows had made an angry shelf on his forehead as he watched the guy hand the wire off to a different man, who wasn't wearing a ring.

"This might be cold," the camera guy said, smooth as velvet near my ear.

"It's fine," I said, twisting to try to watch as he connected the wires and plugged them into a small sound box that would tuck into my slacks. He went to connect the box to the waistband, but Greyson stopped him,

"I can do it, or I'm sure Ms. Thomas can handle this part."

Because I was feeling prickly and petty, I said, "Yes, I think my boyfriend would appreciate if I did it myself."

Greyson's eyes snapped to mine, his lips thinning, and that look was exactly why I'd used the term "boyfriend."

There was a war going on between us that hadn't slowed, hadn't waned, and certainly hadn't ended. He'd shoved his fiancée in my face way back when; the least I could do was shove a fake one in his.

"Okay, we're all set."

And just like that, the cameras were ready for us.

2

KELLY

"OH, MY WORD." Selah laughed into her glass of wine. The evening's entertainment was provided by me, via sacrificing my pride and telling the table about my television debut. Actually, they'd seen it. It had aired during the five-o'clock news segment, which Bryan, my brother-in-law, watched religiously. So, while I was heading back home to change and get ready for my date, they had all been gathered around the television, watching as I embarrassed myself.

"I can't stop watching it," she said, dragging her finger backward on the tablet near her plate. She'd brought up the website and had watched the segment at least fifty times since I arrived.

"It's not that funny," I murmured, sipping from my own glass.

"Sorry, I have to agree with your sister on this—it's hilarious," my date, Jonathan, said, hunching over the tablet to watch it once again. There went my sister's dream of Jonathan and me being a cute married couple and us all vacationing together. So far, he'd asked if I still had the shirt, if I knew Greyson Knox personally, if I could set up a meeting for him, and if I wanted to head back to his place. That was all before dinner even started.

"This part, right here," Selah wheezed, tilting the screen toward me.

It was the scene where the cameraman asked about my connection with Greyson, his deep voice filling the room as he asked, "So, Kelly, there's a rumor going around about a feud between the Knox family and yours...do you have any comments about that? How do you plan to bury the hatchet so the two of you can work together?"

In the image, I glower. It seemed like I was angry at the question, but in reality, the overhead light was in my eyes and I couldn't see shit. Greyson, being taller, wasn't as affected, so he nudged my arm and joked about it.

"I think we're both ready to bury whatever bad blood there is between our families and move on." I didn't agree. In fact, I only glowered harder. It was awkward and weird, for everyone.

The thing is, I hadn't even had a chance to prepare for this meeting. I hadn't had time to prepare my heart for seeing Greyson again, and after four years, I had gotten entirely too comfortable with not being around him. Suddenly, I was thrown into the deep end and told to figure it the fuck out.

"So, what is the beef between you two?" Jonathan asked, sipping from his fifth beer. I certainly hoped he had a designated driver because it sure as hell wouldn't be me.

"It's a long story," Selah answered for me, eyeing me warily. Sitting forward, she flipped the cover on the tablet closed and focused on her plate, likely realizing what this was doing to me. I didn't talk about Greyson Knox, their family, or what they'd done to me.

The silence that followed my sister's statement was full of awkwardness and a big fat reminder that there was a reason I didn't date, at least not the people my sister tried to set me up with. Inevitably, there was always an awkward lull. I wasn't the most socially adept person, and I didn't like the conversation to rely on me, not ever.

Thankfully, my phone rang, and since I was desperate to talk to Aubrey, I jumped up to grab it.

"Hello?" I pushed my finger into my opposite ear on instinct.

"Kelly?" Aubrey asked in a panic. *Oh, thank God.*

"Aubrey, hey…yeah it's me." I let out a heavy sigh and walked down the hall to the office.

"I'm so sorry about the miscommunication! I was out of service all day and didn't get any of your messages until I got back to the hotel." She huffed, sounding winded. The tiny surge of irritation I held for her started to dissipate.

"Are you guys traveling somewhere?" I sat down on the small couch and tried to take comfort in the fact that my sister's children were currently downstairs.

"Yeah, we're in Australia, visiting some of Chance's family. Again, I am so sorry about what happened, and your shirt… I'm assuming something happened, right?"

Heat hit my face as I contemplated how that must have looked to my boss. "Aub, I am so sorry. I spilled my coffee on my shirt right as I got in and I had no time to find anything, so I stole the volunteer's shirt." I groaned into my hands.

Laughter met me as Aubrey began to recount my television segment to someone in the background, presumably Chance. "I'm so sorry, Kelly. I don't mean to laugh, but it's hilarious."

"It's not," I muttered.

"It kind of is. Gosh, from now on, I'm emailing you directly—not that your assistant did a bad job, but that way it's one less person in between us," Aubrey said, her laughter finally transforming into a bit of a sigh.

"It's fine, but what on earth is the story with Greyson Knox? He showed up, did the segment, and then took off." I picked at a pillow in my lap, hearing loud childlike shouts starting to make their way up the stairs. I had very limited time before my nephews found me.

Aubrey let out a yawn as she tried to break it down for me. "I don't know all the specifics, but he wanted to help, and since his family is so famous, I figured it could be really good publicity for the shelter."

"You know the shelter isn't solely on your shoulders, Aub." I'd tried to remind her of that fact a thousand times. She had helped open the facility but wasn't solely responsible for it; still, after she left and then everyone who had helped open it vacated the area, she felt responsible for it. Regardless of the fact that she had started helping with a local shelter near Hermosa Beach, she'd taken up the reins of the Park Street Animal Shelter the second she heard it was going to close its doors.

"I know, but it's needed in that area. There are so many animals that need homes, and I couldn't just leave it. You saved the day, Kelly. I am forever grateful to you for stepping in." Aubrey finished with another yawn, and my nephews were getting closer.

"Let's talk later this week, or email me with updates, okay?"

"Okay, talk soon." She hung up right as my three nephews bolted through the office door, hitting me with Nerf darts.

"Really, Zane?" I grabbed my eye, narrowing my good one on my five-year-old nephew.

"You're the enemy." He shrugged and ran back through the door.

I went to join the adults to finish dinner and get home as soon as possible, all the while turning over ideas in my head about what Aubrey had said.

"Oh good, you're back," my sister said, sitting up. She eyed Jonathan, silently pushing him to say something to me, but he was looking down at his cell. I didn't mind; I doubted this little date was going anywhere anyway.

Once we finished and said our goodbyes, I grabbed an Uber home. Temecula wasn't a massive city, so the bus I took in the mornings was about the size of a smallish RV instead of a long city bus you'd find in a larger town.

Temecula was nestled close to the wine country in California. Spanish-style homes, beautifully manicured lawns, and reno-vated buildings adorned the town. I, however, had settled into an older brick building that was part of the historic district downtown. Walking into my building, you'd assume you were lost in an old Western movie, or a museum, depending on how creative of a person you were. The glass doors were covered in old barnwood, making it look authentically western, and the interior was faded, adorned with leather and abandoned saddles, oil painted pictures of cowboys, and sunsets decorating the walls.

Don't even ask.

The interior of the apartments, however, were updated, modern, and actually pretty damn cute. There were sixteen units tucked away inside, and only rarely did we have to actually go in through the lobby. The tenants had a separate entrance that was much less dramatic, in the back.

My car was currently in the shop. It was a regular thing now every few months or so, and I was afraid it was slowly making its way to an early demise. I'd need to start looking for a new one soon, but with the new job and now Greyson Knox, when would I find the time? Once outside my building, I trudged upstairs and finally let the weight of the day settle into my bones.

I took a bath to try to exorcise the shame and weariness of the day, but even afterward, it hung over my head like a wet cloud.

Greyson Knox was back in my orbit, and with him came the oppression and anger that usually followed. He remembered our deal. For some reason, him acknowledging it felt so much worse than him breaking it had.

But that also meant he'd knowingly accepted the vet position, breaking our deal on purpose. I stood from the couch and stomped toward my desk. It sat under a large window that faced the street below. I grabbed a legal pad, pulled the cap off a ballpoint pen, and settled back into the couch.

Titling the top of the page, I bit down on my lip and got to work.

Raising money for and awareness of the shelter without using Greyson Knox or his big fat wallet

Step one: fire Greyson

Step two: raise five thousand dollars so Aubrey doesn't mind that I fired Greyson.

Step three: start rumor that Greyson Knox has a small penis and syphilis.

I ripped the page out and crumpled it into a small ball.

"This is stupid," I mused out loud. Aubrey wanted Greyson because he brought attention to the animal shelter. If I could find some other way to bring attention to the shelter and raise money without him, I'd be in the clear to fire him without anyone batting an eye.

Suddenly, I had a plan.

I would execute it first thing in the morning.

3

KELLY

"Morning, Kel." My neighbor Jones smiled at me, lifting his travel mug to his lips, and I gave him a brittle smile in return. No one called me Kel. I'd never given him permission to do so, and honestly, I barely even knew the guy. He would talk to me, flirting with me every chance he found, but he gave me serious Joe Goldberg stalker vibes, so I never encouraged him.

"Morning, Jones. Hope you have a nice day." I power-walked toward the stairs because getting stuck inside an elevator with him was low on my list of priorities.

Today I was wearing my favorite outfit: tight black pencil skirt, white low scoop-neck tank, black blazer capped at the elbows, and my favorite wedges. My hair was curled, my makeup was on point, and my confidence was next level.

I'd slept listening to a motivational YouTube video, woken with the sunrise, and felt like a heavyweight champion about to box my enemy for the title.

I walked into the shelter before anyone else even arrived, and it made me feel like a million bucks. I was finally, *finally* on top of this new job.

"Hey, wait! Watch out——" someone shouted at me, right as my ankle twisted to the left and I fell flat on my face. My coffee slid ahead of me on the laminate flooring, the lid popping off, brown liquid bursting everywhere.

I lay there, unsure of what had just happened, right as Greyson walked around the corner, wearing a pair of light green scrubs.

"Sorry, tried to warn you." He bent down, lending me a hand to help me up. I swatted it away and crawled to my knees, slowly making my way back to standing.

"What the hell did I slip on?" I slowly looked down while pushing my locks back, desperate to hide my reddening face.

"Uh, I let the cats out a little early so they could run around, and one of them puked on the floor. I was on my way back to grab some cleaning supplies as you walked in."

Right.

I cleared my throat. "So, I slipped on…"

"Cat vomit," Greyson finished for me.

"I…" I tried to speak, but words weren't coming. That meant I had cat puke on my favorite outfit. My coffee was gone, and I once again had no spare clothes. Why did I even bother?

I heard a small sound of what I could only decipher as laughter from the man standing next to me. My eyes swung to Greyson's, and sure enough, he was holding back tears due to how hard he wanted to laugh.

"This isn't funny," I declared, grabbing for my purse. All the contents had slid across the floor, and my favorite lipstick was in the puddle of cat puke.

"I'm not laughing at you," Greyson wheezed.

"You are," I countered.

"I'm just laughing in general, at the room, at nothing in particular." He raised a shoulder, his blue eyes dancing with amusement.

"Did you do this on purpose?" I accused, sidestepping the close proximity he claimed next to me.

"Did I what?" He sobered, narrowing his eyes.

"You heard me. It's not the first time you've pulled something like this." I crossed my arms, ignoring the tampon that had landed next to my foot. *Shit.*

Greyson's forehead wrinkled, his eyebrows pulling in tight. "No, I didn't fucking force the cat to puke so you'd walk in it."

He scoffed, gave me a death glare, and walked away.

Whatever.

I had a mess to clean up and a plan to execute.

It was finished. I had brainstormed all day, with graphs, highlighter pens, and sticky notes. I had a plan to raise money, all without Greyson Knox being at the shelter. I did a victory dance while my assistant Julie eyed me, confused and suspicious.

She didn't understand why I wanted to fire the guy. He'd brought in donuts for the entire staff and volunteers by day two. I hadn't even learned everyone's name yet.

She was a Greyson fan, as was Payton and nearly everyone else. Fine, but we didn't need him, so I would fire him before any long-term damage could be done with staff morale.

I cleared my throat. "Julie, could you please ask Mr. Knox to come into my office?"

She let out a sigh. "You're going to fire him wearing that?"

I looked down at my hot pink track suit. The ass said *Juicy*, and the zip-up jacket had the little squirting water emoji printed over the breast pocket. I had purchased it at the swap meet across the street. It was faster than getting an Uber back home just to come all the way back.

I waved a hand in the air. "It's fine. Would you mind dropping my outfit off at the drycleaners? Then treat yourself to some lunch." I handed over my card and smiled. I liked Julie.

Technically, I shouldn't even have had an assistant, but Aubrey insisted that I did. She had found some room in our nearly nonexistent budget, and I hoped we could keep her, because she was really good at keeping me grounded.

"Okay." Julie let out a heavy sigh, pulling a pencil from the mountain of frizz on her head.

I cleared my desk of all fundraising plans and steepled my fingers, readying myself for Greyson. I hadn't seen or talked to him again after the whole cat vomit incident. He stayed in his area of the shelter and I stayed in my office, unless I needed to talk to the staff or get coffee from the kitchen.

A knock on my door had my spine stiffening, straight as an arrow.

"Come in," I called out, mentally adding some kind of resolute firmness to my tone.

Greyson walked in, still wearing his scrubs. I felt the smallest bit of butterflies take flight in my stomach at how the soft material made him seem vulnerable, something about seeing him out of those power suits his father dressed him in…

"Thank you for coming. Please take a seat," I said as fire licked at my insides. This was my first firing; I had never even witnessed one before. I briefly recalled the way Aubrey had tried to turn Chance down in a professional manner when he requested her services as his lawyer.

She was firm and no-nonsense. She'd had a past with the guy, but she still hadn't faltered, so neither would I.

"I have been going over some paperwork regarding our finances and any places that could use tightening up." I laid my fingers flat on the desk and hated that Greyson's blue eyes tracked the movement.

His jaw grew tight as though he knew where this was headed. *Good.*

"Sorry, Mr. Knox, but it doesn't look like this arrangement is going to work out. I appreciate your efforts, and this is in no way a reflection of your work or skills." I was totally bullshitting him; for whatever reason, there weren't any files whatsoever on his salary. His resume was visible, but nothing else. So, I was lying through my teeth, but I knew he must be getting a decent wage.

I mean, he was a veterinarian, and not just any rando either. He was *Greyson Knox*. His father was the head of one of the most prestigious law firms in the country. He had an entire generation of rich, asshole successors lined up behind that name, and everyone in California drooled over the chance to be in the same room as one.

"Are you serious right now?" Greyson laughed, running a hand over the day-old stubble that lined his jaw.

I blinked, summoned as many Aubrey vibes as I could, and sat taller. "I am serious, Mr. Kn—"

"Call me Mr. Knox again and I will show you my interpretation of you using that term of endearment with me." His eyes flashed with that violent lust I used to live for.

"It's not a term of endearment," I stammered awkwardly.

In a swift movement, Greyson was out of his chair and leaning over the desk, looking down at me. "It is very much a term of endearment, Kat, so don't test me, or I will lay out in graphic detail what I will do to your body if you say it again."

Blink. Swallow. Wheeze.

"P…please take a seat, Greyson."

I wouldn't touch that stick of dynamite he'd just thrown between us, not even if there was heat simmering in my belly, begging me to move toward it.

His eyes searched mine before he slowly lowered himself back down.

"Look, I don't think this is a good arrangement, and I know financially—"

"There you go again with the big words," he joked, shaking his head back and forth. It stopped me, because the look in his eye said he had a secret and I would be the one feeling left out once it was spilled.

"Here's a fun little tidbit of info for you, Kat…" He leaned forward, a grin so wide and perfect claiming his face. "You can't fire me."

That made my chest feel hollow, like a kiddie bat had just smacked me there, stinging and irritating.

"What do you mean exactly?"

His lean frame inched closer, letting me smell his delicious cologne: spicy, sweet, heady.

"I'm not an employee. As you know, I don't legally have my license of veterinary medicine yet."

I didn't know that. Shit, I needed to do more research on animal things.

"I've been given the green light to volunteer my time, free of charge, while reporting to my mentor, Dr. Santé, who can vouch for my surgery skills. The camera crew is for the YouTube channel I agreed to set up for the shelter, and it will double as an introductory video for incoming vet school students attending UC Davis. Check my contract—your boss made sure this was a mutually beneficial arrangement."

He smirked, straightened, and walked out of my office.

Well shit.

4

GREYSON

"Hey, what's good?" my best friend asked, exhaling heavily into the phone. I could picture him, a joint hanging from the side of his mouth, his legs bent, his ass planted on a dirty piece of asphalt, likely ruining whatever thousand-dollar suit he was stuffed in.

I smiled at the image, because I'd have been right there next to him smoking, ruining my suit too, if I could. Josh was his father's puppet for the time being, but just like me, he was slowly hatching a plan to get free.

"I'm here...moved in, started the gig," I droned, like they were just facts I was reading off a sheet of paper instead of the monumental decisions that had led to me dropping my father, his firm, and the entire billion-dollar birthright, and becoming a small-town vet.

"Fucking Doctor Dolittle over there." Josh laughed into my ear, and it made me smile.

"It works. Animals may shit sometimes, but they never do it on the people they love." I pulled out my college shirt, yanking it

28

on over my head. I had just moved into my townhouse, and the only things unpacked were my bed and the TV.

"And Kat?" my best friend asked carefully.

I hesitated, walking down the stairs and nearly tripping over a box. "She's the manager of the shelter, just like I thought."

"Fuuuuuckkkk. Oh to have been a fly on the wall when she saw you." He chuckled.

Asshole.

"It wasn't all sunshine and butterflies, I can tell you that much." I pushed past the pinching in my chest at the memory of her reaction to seeing me.

"You guys talk about things yet?" Josh sounded concerned for me. Deep down, he was a good guy…a professional bullshitter, yes, but when it mattered, he was loyal as hell.

"No. She tried to fire me yesterday." I grabbed for a glass out of a box that was sitting on the ledge of my counter, and again I ignored how much it hurt that she had already tried to get rid of me.

"Shit, man." He laughed. "Well, you're there for a reason. Don't forget that…you knew it wouldn't be easy."

I scoffed, walking toward the fridge. "Thanks. It's hard sometimes to remember why I consciously walked back to the one woman who ripped my heart out."

I tried to laugh, but it died on my tongue. Josh didn't laugh either.

"Because she's the only one who ever made it beat in the first place, man. True love and all that shit. It's worth it, right?"

I eyed the picture on my fridge, pinned in place with a simple black magnet, and let out a heavy sigh. "Yeah…it is."

5

KELLY

Okay, new plan. The previous day's botched firing had been embarrassing, to say the least. Today, I needed to think on my feet, get some more background information—hit him where it hurt. I had started the morning full of confidence, and then I went to start my car. Damn thing wouldn't even turn over, which indicated a dead battery. I didn't even have the energy to be angry that I'd just paid upwards of five hundred dollars to have it serviced and fixed.

Undeterred by having to catch the bus, I stormed into the shelter like a warlord would his castle—if that warlord had to check for cat vomit, that is. Payton was there, setting up her station at the desk, checking the log, and booting up the computer. I smiled and headed toward my office, hoping the vet wasn't in yet.

I shouldered in through my office door, my stomach a jittery mess, and stopped mid-step. There was a massive bouquet of flowers on my desk, a small box next to it, and a venti-sized coffee waiting for me.

I dropped my laptop bag and purse then shuffled back out toward the front.

"Uh, Payton...did someone get the wrong office for a delivery?"

Her honey-colored hair flew to the side as she swiveled in her chair. "No idea...I haven't seen any delivery guys come in yet this morning."

She swiveled back toward her screen, ignoring my furrowed brows and pinched face.

Carefully, I sauntered back to my desk, hunting for a card. Internally, I begged for it not to be from Jones, my neighbor. His stalker vibes had been really strong in the elevator earlier, and although I had never told him where I worked, I knew he likely knew, especially if he was like Joe from that book, *You*.

I pulled open the attached note and read the inscription.

Kelly,

This is just a thank you for all you're doing. Chance and I couldn't be more grateful that you're there keeping things going. We both grew pretty attached to those animals.

Love, Aubrey

I let out the tightly wound breath that had nearly strangled me and relaxed in my chair. I'd have to call her later to say thank you. For some, strange, unwarranted reason, I'd wondered for just half a second if the arrangement could have been from Greyson, which would have been impossible...but in the recesses of my mind, the thought was there just the same.

I'd have to get really practiced at shoving away those thoughts and pushing them down as far as I could.

Sipping the warm coffee and digging through the box of chocolates, I got to work.

My schedule was up, telling me everything Julie had planned for me. I mentally added each thing to the list that endlessly went on and on in my head. Everything looked easy enough, clear enough, except one chunk of time.

Confused again, for the second time that morning, I called Julie.

"Good morning, boss!" she chirped happily.

"Morning, Jules. Hey…"

"Morning," she said to someone in the background, sounding distracted. Where the hell was she, and why wasn't she at work?

"Julie?" I tried to regain her attention.

"Kelly, I'm here! Sorry, there are so many people here today, a few friends I haven't seen in forever." Her voice was muffled again as she yelled, "Hey! Yes, call me sometime—let's get lunch."

"Julie! I need to talk to you," I snapped, immediately feeling like shit for doing so.

"Geez, chill out, boss. What's up?"

I inhaled through my nose and exhaled through my mouth. "First of all, I'm sorry for yelling. I shouldn't have done that. Second of all, where are you right now?"

She laughed. "It's all good, boss. I'm at my yoga session. Aubrey said it would be fine as long as I was in by nine on Thursdays and Fridays. Oh, and did you get those flowers?

Aubrey had me deliver them this morning before my session started."

"Yes, I did, thank you," I said, biting back my retort about her scheduling her yoga time into her contract to work here.

"So, what did you need?"

Shaking myself out of my reverie, I recovered, saying, "Sorry, I just had a question about something you scheduled for me."

"Is this about the three-o'clock appointment?" She yelled hello at someone in the background again. I was losing her.

"Kind of. It's scheduled like an appointment, but in the notes it says VTEXRM...what do those letters mean?"

"Ohhhh yeah, sorry about that. I created my own code thing. It's vet, exam room," she explained, like that cleared it up.

"And what does that mean?"

"Dr. Knox said he wanted your help on a surgery this afternoon. His camera crew is coming in again and wanted to film it. We're getting some really big donors now that he's here."

I wanted to shoot back that I'd arrived around the same time so it could be me bringing them in. No one knew for sure.

"Okay, thanks Julie. Appreciate it."

She said goodbye, and I was left staring at my screen in confusion.

"Knock-knock," Greyson said while opening my office door.

Irritation bubbled in my chest. "That does not count as a knock."

He smirked. "Okay. Good, you got your coffee. Wasn't sure how you took it, but I remember you liking—"

"You got this for me?"

He blinked and shoved his hands into his pockets. In the past, that move had indicated that he was nervous or shy; now, I had no idea.

"Yeah, since I kind of ruined yours for you yesterday."

It hadn't technically been his fault, but I was glad to hear him take the blame.

Just the same, pride surged forward like a puppeteer, moving me like a marionette. I turned and threw the rest of the deliciously hot coffee in the trash.

He watched, tracking my movements with no expression on his face.

Because I was nothing to him, just a blip on his radar, a regret...someone I was sure he wished wasn't here.

"Next time, don't bother. I don't want anything from you," I bitterly declared, staring at my laptop screen.

He was there in the room, but I wasn't focused on him, so I had no idea what he was doing.

"I seem to remember there were a few things I had to offer that you couldn't refuse." Those perfect lips slung to the side in the form of a smirk. Old hurt flourished inside, like a current of air hitting a flame, bringing it back to life.

You just couldn't refuse, could you?

The words he'd used to accuse me on the day we broke up came crashing back into my head, tumbling down into my heart, reminding me why I hated this man. He was vicious and cruel.

"There isn't anything you'd ever be able to offer that I'd have a hard time refusing. Anything that ever existed between us is over," I snapped, so grateful that I had already trashed his coffee gift.

His smirk fell into a flat line, his eyebrows forming a shelf on that handsome face of his. It made me feel triumphant, even if it did come with a small slice of guilt. I didn't like hurting him, but he'd hurt *me*.

"I didn't mean it like that," he said coldly, shoving his hands back into his pockets.

Sure you didn't.

Not my fault he was just now realizing the last time he'd said those words to me.

"Don't care," I said snidely, clicking around in my inbox.

"Kat, I didn't…it's…fuck." He exhaled heavily. His off-kilter comment made me feel like a hot iron had been placed inside my ribcage.

Why do I care that he looks defeated right now?

"I meant that time, the one where you laughed about not being able to refuse me…do you remember that?" he asked, his blue eyes begging me to remember what was running around in his mind.

A carefully tucked away memory came floating back, hot and heavy as I remembered him slamming his lips against mine, grabbing me by the thighs, carrying me to a nearby wall. He'd asked if he could have me that night, even though I was mad at him. We'd fought, but he had bought me my favorite takeout and watched my favorite movie then tried to kiss me. After his second kiss, I laughed into his neck, saying I could never refuse him.

Heat overwhelmed my face as I cleared my throat and moved away from him. Why would he bring that up? He wasn't playing fair; weren't our memories a part of our promise to stay away from one another? Wasn't there some code here where we couldn't remember the sexual times of our relationship while in the same room?

He smirked, standing tall, like he'd just won this round. "I look forward to your help in my surgery later this afternoon...you might want to be sure you have on comfortable clothing."

His parting words left me glaring at my office door as it closed.

Lord help me.

―――――

"Hey girl," Aubrey said, smiling at her laptop screen. She was beautiful as always, her face dotted with more freckles than I remembered her ever having.

"Hey, you look happy...and tan." I smiled at her, leaning my chin in my open palm.

"We spend nearly every day outside here, and Australia is hot."

Oh yeah...it was summer over there; of course she was out in the sun and tan from it. A pang of jealousy ran through me, quick and sharp. It was the same feeling I got when I saw my sister smile at her husband or laugh with him. It was this fear that I wouldn't ever find that kind of happiness. Seeing Chance walk by and grip the ends of Aubrey's hair then release them quickly only amplified the feeling.

"How's that baby bean doing?" I asked, hoping she'd show me her belly.

She and Chance were expecting their first child in a few months, and I hated that I wasn't there to see her belly grow.

"Baby is healthy and strong and kicking me all the freaking time." She laughed, lowering her camera view so I could see her swollen midsection. She wore a tight black tank that more than highlighted her roundness.

"It looks like a basketball is in there." I smiled, getting closer to the screen.

"I know, that's what I always tell Chance. I never knew that it legit would look like I had stuffed a Spalding ball under my shirt." Aubrey looked over her shoulder briefly then drew her eyes back to me. "Kel, I have to get going soon, but I wanted to check in and see how things are going with the new vet?" Her eyes grew tight with what was probably concern.

"All good over here. In fact"—I held up a pair of scrubs—"I'm helping in a surgery this afternoon." I smiled like I was proud when really, I felt like I was sinking.

"That's amazing!" Aubrey beamed.

"Not to rat anyone out, but you are aware that he's not techni-cally a licensed vet, right?" I just wanted to be sure she knew, and if she happened to think we should fire him and look for someone else, that was her choice.

"Oh yeah, about that…" Aubrey narrowed her eyes, sitting up in her chair. "Dr. Santé, I think that's his name…anyway, he's been in touch with me, letting me know that Greyson has been reporting to him, goes over surgeries and whatever else with him." She waved her hand away like it was nothing. There went my big chance to have him fired.

"Oh, great." I feigned a pleased demeanor.

"This is why you were the perfect choice for this position—your willingness to get in there and know all the facts. I am so excited to see the footage the news crew gets from it." She brought her hands together, clapping excitedly.

"Should be fun." I faux-beamed, hoping to move this along. I appreciated her checking in, but I knew I was being immature about Greyson and I hated that I was reacting to him at all.

"Okay, well keep me posted on everything, okay?"

"Will do." I smiled and pressed the end button on our chat. Letting out a heavy sigh, I stood and headed for the door.

I could do this. I could assist on a surgery and not make it weird. Helping sew up a cat sounded harmless enough, and that was what Julie had put in my notes. I pictured a tiny, small cat and considered how that would go.

I still had about twenty minutes before I was expected in the surgery, so I took off toward the side yard of the shelter where we let the dogs play. There were tons of ramps and tunnels for them to run through, tons of toys for them to chew on. I loved coming to the yard because the dogs were always so happy.

It was slightly chilly for January in California, mostly rainy and gross, but the air didn't hold much of a bite. Still, it was gloomy. I scanned the yard for the tuft of black fur I had come to enjoy whenever I found my way out here.

Since my first day on the job, I had found comfort in talking with some of the pets at the shelter. I didn't have many friends in Temecula. After everything that had gone down four years earlier, I had the tendency to be a bit guarded when it came to friendships.

Aubrey once told me I was like a sharpshooter, ready to fire but aware that I didn't always have to. Either way, I was guarding and protecting that wall.

I hadn't ever been overly affectionate toward pets, but when I first met Jet, he'd put his head in my lap and watched me with big brown eyes while I spilled all my concerns over the new job to him.

I went back the next day, and the day after; I even came to see him over the weekend. He was becoming a big part of why I loved this job. I had toyed with the idea of adopting him, but when I'd brought up the idea gently to my landlord, it was met with harsh and firm denial.

"No pets. Not even a hamster. Never." That's what Mr. Gruin had said in his thick Russian accent.

I couldn't lose my place, not in this rental market.

So, I spent as much time as I could with Jet in the shelter. Since I'd never been attached to animals, it was a new sensation to feel excited about seeing that wagging tail and that dark head dip up and down when Jet saw me. It was exhilarating having something to look forward to every day.

I ducked down as I came across Jet's space, unlocking his door. Kneeling, I threw my arms open and let the bundle of energy walk into my embrace.

"Hey buddy, how are you?" I kissed the top of Jet's head.

From what I had read in his file, he was part Lab, part Mastiff, so he drooled a ton but had the kindest eyes and the sweetest nature. He'd come to the shelter three months earlier, during the transition from Chance and Aubrey leaving, the other partners backing out, and all the shuffling that had occurred. No one really knew much about him except that he had been found digging through trash cans in back alleys and so malnourished his ribs were showing.

He licked the side of my face, making me shift back onto my heels.

"I know, I was supposed to be here this morning, but I got caught up with work. Why don't I come by later on my break and we'll go for a walk?" I rubbed his belly.

My heart felt so full whenever I was near him. Sometimes when I stayed late at work, I'd bring him into my office, kick off my shoes, and let him curl up around my toes.

Looking up at the wall clock, I realized I was going to be late helping with the surgery if I didn't get moving. "I'll come see you in a bit."

I kissed his head once more and closed his space back up.

Heading down the hall and cutting across a few hallways, I moved toward the back where we had a workspace set up for giving animals shots and bathing them. It was a large area with three metal tables in the middle, a large bath and shower off to one side, and a few pet dryers aligned with the kennels, built into the wall. It was nicely organized, with laminate flooring and soft grey accent walls.

Jamie, one of the staff members, smiled at me as she prepped what looked like a shot of some kind. There were a few metal instruments laid out in front of her as well, along with a pair of gloves, a mask, and a gown.

It was freezing in the room, forcing me to rub my hands together. I was dressed in green scrubs; they were thin, too big, and no help against the temperature in the room.

"Hey, you ready?" Greyson asked, smirking at me. He was wearing a pair of scrubs like mine, but his were a thick material that fit him perfectly, almost like they were tailored for him. With his blonde hair and tan skin, he looked…*really fucking good*.

"I'm ready," I replied quietly, moving toward the box of gloves. The door opened, revealing the camera crew all flooding the room with their equipment and boom sticks.

I tried to quell the feeling of unease bubbling in my stomach as they got set up. I didn't want to think about being on the news again.

"Kelly, come on over here beside me. This is going to be pretty easy. I will tell you exactly what to do, and you'll just follow my lead, okay?" Greyson raised an eyebrow, making sure I was ready.

I nodded my head, watching the side door for Jamie to walk in with the little cat carrier.

Greyson let out a little laugh as he put his mask on. "I hope you stretched today."

My eyes jumped to him in question right as the door opened and the sound of squealing echoed through the room. The camera crew got into place quickly as Greyson moved toward the door, meeting Jamie, who was grasping a leash.

My eyes went wide as I took in the creature following her.

"No," I gasped.

Greyson's gaze swung to mine, and he briefly hesitated but plowed forward as he asked, "You aren't backing out, are you?"

I took a few steps backward. I couldn't take my eyes off the pink and black hairy thing waddling toward us.

"No." I shook my head, moving to hide behind the table.

"Oh come on, Kel...you can handle a tiny little surgery on a harmless pig."

Harmless. Ha!

A delicate memory surfaced of when I'd shared my utter and horrific fear of pigs with Greyson. I was drunk at the time, snuggled under a blanket with him. We were playing some form of truth or dare, and I didn't want to move, so I kept picking truth.

I had been trampled as a kid by four huge pigs when I went to visit my aunt up in Oregon. They had no idea I had never been around pigs, or alone inside a pig pen.

I was only seven, with little twig arms and shorter than half my class. I had three stitches in my left leg that served as a reminder to steer clear of pigs and farms.

I would have glared at Greyson for pulling this, but I refused to take my eyes off the pig that was walking strangely.

It lifted its nose in the air as Greyson bent low to pat its head. He turned the animal, revealing the pig's enlarged stomach. There was a massive growth coming from its undercarriage.

"Tumor?" I asked, trying not to feel sorry for the evil thing, but it looked painful.

Greyson kept his gaze on the pig. "Yeah...it's grown rapidly, and if we don't get it out soon, she's going to die."

My heart wilted a little—but not enough to touch it.

"Kat, can you please hand me that needle to your left?" Greyson asked, still petting the animal. I swallowed my anxiety, hyperaware of the camera pointed at my back.

"Please stop calling me that," I quietly muttered to the vet at my side. I didn't want any pet names, no nicknames, nothing between us. I handed him the needle and stepped back. The pig grunted, slowly trying to lower herself to the ground.

Greyson injected the pig, continuing to pat its belly, murmuring something soft and sweet into its ear. My stomach flipped and dipped at the sight of it. My mind went back to dark nights when I was tucked into the crook of his arm and he'd whisper sweet things to me in between kisses.

His dark eyes moved up to where I stood frozen, watching him.

"You ready to help me lift her?" The side of his lip turned up in a mocking glare.

"Um…" The dryness in my throat caused it to tighten.

Lift the pig? Touch the pig? No, I can't do that.

"Isn't that thing like three hundred pounds or something?" I deflected, hoping he wouldn't notice that I was sweating.

"No. She's not." He laughed, as if he were hiding a secret. "Besides, she's in a sling—just grab the ends and help me lift." He moved toward the head of the pig.

My feet were rooted to the ground. He did not honestly expect me to lift this pig with him, did he?

"Come on, Kat." His eyes bounced toward the cameras behind me.

Oh my god.

He was challenging me. He was getting me back for trying to fire him, the son of a bitch. He was testing to see if I would follow through for the publicity and the donors we needed, or if I would chicken out.

I bent down, gripping the poles, and readied myself to lift. Greyson's light brown eyebrows jumped to his forehead as I moved into position.

"On three." He locked his eyes on me.

Please no. "Okay."

"One, two, three, lift." Greyson grunted something as I lifted the poles. In my head, things were going perfectly.

My eyes were closed, so as to better picture this imaginary strength and nerves of steel. I had an irregular fear of pigs, but I was going to lift this one if it was the last thing I did.

Except the strength never came. My eyes flew open as Greyson yelled, "Watch out! Kelly, keep her stable!"

My feet got caught underneath me, forcing me to trip backward toward the camera crew, who were all scrambling to get out of the way as I landed on my ass, taking the full weight of the pig on my torso.

I made some garbled sound from my chest before all the air left it.

I was going to die.

"Help!" I panted to the cameramen towering over me.

"Oh shit!" someone half-yelled, half-murmured beside me. There was an obnoxious light in my face from above, probably from the camera equipment, and it made seeing anything nearly impossible.

Finally, a pair of hands came under the beast on my chest, the knuckles grazing my breasts while they tried to find purchase on the animal. Once the weight was gone, I turned on my side and started coughing.

"Sorry about that…at my old clinic, we had an electronic gurney that we used for larger animals, but seeing as this pig is only eighty pounds, I figured it wouldn't be a big deal to just lift her between the two of us." Greyson narrowed his gaze on me, sitting in a crouched position, his scrubs stretching across his knees.

I could hear light snickering above me, the evil cameramen still filming, of course, never missing a moment, I'm sure.

I sat up, got to my feet, and brushed my hands on my scrubs.

"Under normal circumstances, I'm sure that would have been the case." I gave Greyson a death glare. "However, considering my debilitating fear of pigs, I think I literally went weak in the knees."

A confused frown worked itself across Greyson's handsome face. "Oh…"

He said it in a tone that made it seem like he had totally forgotten about that, but I knew better. I knew he remembered that night; he was just being his normal vicious self.

He moved on to one of the volunteers who were poking around near the door in case we needed extra hands. "Would you mind stepping in and helping me? Seems our director isn't able to…" His eyes met mine before glancing back toward the cameras. "Help with certain animals."

My face was on fire. Jamie moved around me, putting on a pair of gloves and helping Greyson with the pig. I just stood there watching as the cameramen kept filming. He'd just made me look like I shouldn't be the director, like I shouldn't be the one looking after these animals, bearing responsibility for their lives.

Fuck, maybe I shouldn't.

Raw emotions began to tug inside, as though an invisible person was in my chest trying to untangle an unruly knot. Memories of a time Greyson had made a fool of me in the past surfaced, forcing my feet to move toward the door. Pushing past the camera crew, keeping my eyes to the ground, I quickly rounded the corner into my office, where I shut the door and locked myself inside.

My fingers itched to write to Aubrey and explain that this was a mistake, that I wasn't cut out for this. I knew I was just helping them out, but what I thought might be me finding my place in Temecula outside of being an assistant had just flopped on the ground like a water balloon in the heat of summer.

I was an imposter coasting on someone else's dream, and now Greyson was here to call my bluff.

6

GREYSON

"Why am I shoving laundry off this chair like I'm walking through a frat house?" my father asked in a tone that fluctuated between disapproval and disgust.

I let out a sigh, moving through the room to the window, where I watched the rain pelt against it in heavy thuds.

"Greyson, did you hear me?"

Another sigh battered my lungs. I hadn't been expecting a visit from my father, especially here in my townhouse, a place he'd compared to a large tool shed.

"I heard you, Dad…I'm just choosing to ignore your comment. I just moved in, haven't unpacked yet."

"You wouldn't have to unpack anything if you'd hire a house-keeper, like you were raised with." He huffed.

I turned from the window to take him in. He clutched his coffee mug while he crossed one leg over the other. His rigid shoulders were like two poles on either side of his face, his Tom

Ford jacket rising with his discomfort. It was amusing, him being out of his element.

"Let's skip the pleasantries and jump right to why you're here." I shoved my hands into my pockets, taking a step toward him.

"Why won't you return my calls regarding the firm?"

I blinked, shocked that he was still chasing this conversation.

"I gave my notice—there's no reason to discuss the firm."

"Goddammit, why are you doing this?" He stood, letting his coffee spill to the floor.

I stood where I was, unfazed by the red flushing his face.

"You know why." I crossed my arms.

"Over her?" He pointed a finger at me, his blue eyes flaring.

"Yes, over her. What you did was unforgivable." I tried to control my tone, but the memory of what he'd done to sabotage my relationship surfaced, causing my breath to come in and out in shallow spurts.

"She won't take you back just because you showed up here, pretending to be someone new." He shook his head and turned for the door. With his hand around the knob, he said, "You've had your four years of fun, and all is forgiven if you simply show up at the firm tomorrow morning. You can even still be an animal doctor if you want, just on the side."

He sounded hopeful and so sure of himself, like I'd just done four years of college earning my way toward becoming a vet for nothing.

"It doesn't work like that—I still have at least three years left of school. This isn't a hobby to me. I'm doing this. It's my career now," I assured him, hating how defensive and small it made me feel.

He merely shook his head. "You did this for her, wasted all that time...for her. She won't take you back, but I will. Call me when you've come to your senses." He turned the knob and slammed the door shut behind him.

I tried to shove his words aside, but there was some truth to them that had me lingering, turning them over in my head. After what had happened and what I had done, Kat likely wouldn't take me back, but I had to try.

I hung my head in frustration as the look on her face filled my mind. She had been hurt by the stunt I'd pulled. I'd thought it would be funny, maybe loosen her tight shoulders and help her ease back into a friendship with me. When she mentioned her debilitating fear of pigs, I wanted to kick my own ass. I had forgotten the main point to that pig story she'd told me one night when we'd been drinking.

For some reason, I had it twisted in my mind that she was fond of them, not deathly afraid. I was such a fucking idiot.

I needed to talk to her, make sure she knew I hadn't done it to be mean or cruel.

Grabbing my keys, I headed for the door and rushed downstairs to my car.

7

KELLY

"WHY ARE you doing this to me?" My sister wheezed while clutching her stomach, and I rolled my eyes then shoved her to the floor with my bare foot.

"Aunt Kel pushed Mommy again," my nephew yelled toward his father's office, which had me rolling my eyes again.

"Bunch of tattletales around here," I muttered, eyeing the little five-year-old who scampered off when he caught sight of my glare.

"Sorry, you just...the pig and the footage." My sister wheezed again.

She thought the video was hilarious, downright primetime television worthy. It wasn't. I'd honestly thought the news crew wouldn't post their footage to the shelter's YouTube channel, but when I arrived for dinner at my sister's house, she promptly shoved her phone in my face with the clip of me falling to the ground while she laughed her ass off.

"I'm going to head home." I stood, stretching and wondering why I'd even bothered to come over here tonight...*other than not wanting to be alone.*

"Okay, zipping it." Selah pretended to zip her lips shut.

I eyed her distrustfully before slouching back into her couch.

"So, it's been, what—an entire week? Dish about Knox." The dark tendrils from her messy bun fell in front of her face, covering her green eyes, which matched our mother's.

"Almost a week, yeah." I nodded, shoving a grape into my mouth.

"Has he sent you any lingering stares?" She shimmied her shoulders while reaching for the bowl of fruit.

I let out a laugh and reached for my wine. "Not even close." Although that wasn't entirely true. I had caught him staring at me several times, and each stare was loaded with unspoken words and smothered fire.

"Has he even mentioned the big breakup?" she nervously asked, making that stone in my chest sink farther.

"No, he hasn't. He's only at the shelter for some PR thing, I'm sure. Help the firm's image or get his resume ready for his run for Congress, something like that. Either way, I'm not on his radar. He probably has a six-foot-fifteen girlfriend who eats kale for every meal," I said in a muted rush.

"Don't hate green eaters—they're just living their best lives," Selah warned. She was big on the kale and leafy greens now that she was a mom of three, said she was trying to ensure she lived long enough to get grandbabies.

"Sorry, you know what...I'm actually pretty tired, sis. I'm going to head home."

"Okay, but call me when you get there." She leaned forward, pulling me into a hug.

The last thing I saw was her making a loud pig sound while pulling me nose up to look like a snout. I could hear her laugh echo through the door as I shut it and made my way to the bus station. It wasn't even that the stupid footage was out there—in fact, I'd much rather have it be on the YouTube channel instead of the evening news—but the lingering sting from Greyson's betrayal still hurt.

The bus arrived at the stop closest to my apartment in a mere seven minutes due to it being later in the evening.

I ran up my stairs, only to come to a swift halt at the sight of Greyson sitting against my door, arms flung over his knees, head tipped back with his eyes closed. I carefully stepped toward him, unsure of what he was doing at my door.

As I got closer, he stirred, righting his head and getting to his feet.

"Hey." The dark, husky tone left his chest like it'd been locked up in there all day, just waiting for this moment to be released. His eyes were soft, and gentle…almost like he was vulnerable.

"Were you asleep?" I pointed toward the floor, where he'd just been.

"Yeah, I dozed off a little while ago." He rubbed his neck, blushing.

"How long have you been here?" I asked, moving around him to get into my apartment. For some reason, I didn't want to have this conversation in the hall. I could feel prying eyes on us from the other tenants spying, and if they knew who Greyson was, I'd never hear the end of it.

"Just a while. I didn't realize you'd be out so late." He narrowed his eyes as I turned to usher him into my space.

Shutting the door, I moved to take my coat and shoes off, ignoring how it felt to have him in my home, looking around at everything that made me who I was.

Greyson's gaze cut back to mine then moved slowly down my body, his eyes going wide just after his perfect mouth opened the smallest bit.

Confused, I looked down at myself and...oh. *Oh.*

"Uhhh," I stammered, trying to cover for what I was wearing —not that I needed to, but I didn't want him to think...what didn't I want him to think? I didn't care what he thought.

Selah had asked me to try on this new little number that had come into her shop. I had planned to change before I left her house, but I hadn't even remembered until I was on the bus and getting side eye from an elderly woman. It was a tight, short, black dress with a plunging neckline. I wouldn't normally pick something like it for myself, but it was made out of mate-rial that felt softer than butter. I literally felt like I was in a fluffy cloud all night.

"Hot date tonight?" Greyson cleared his throat, moving to my couch, throwing his body weight down.

"Um...yeah," I lied, walking around him and pulling on a hoodie that was in a big pile of clean clothes on the end of my couch. I had nearly forgotten I'd said I had a boyfriend that first day.

Greyson scoffed, rubbing a hand down his face. "Right. I almost forgot about your *boyfriend.*"

His tone was flat, incredulous, like he didn't believe me.

"Not your business, Knox. What are you doing here?" I pushed past him toward the kitchen. My mind was going a million miles a minute. *Why is he here?* I opened the fridge and rummaged for a yogurt while I internally processed what was going on with him.

He waited a few seconds before answering. It felt like an eternity before he finally let out a sigh and parted those luscious lips.

"I'm here because I want to apologize for the pig incident."

He turned his head, laying his neck against the back of my couch, leaving his scent everywhere, ruining it.

"Apology accepted."

He heaved another sigh and stood up. "No, you don't understand...that night we played truth or dare—we were drinking...do you remember?"

He stalked closer. I eyed my apartment walls, as if they were the problem—too small, too narrow. *Dammit.* That night was one of my favorite nights with him. We'd been dating for months, but that night, he'd wrangled a confession out of me, one I was both ready and not ready to share with him.

"I mixed the story up." His long legs and muscular thighs carried him two steps closer. "I thought you loved them...I thought your face would light up when you saw the thing waddle in."

I backed up against the counter as he moved even closer. My neck was turning red and flames licked at my chest, reminding me that this wasn't a good idea.

"I thought maybe you'd give me a chance."

My breath stalled in lungs. He was so close now; I could smell his expensive cologne wrapping around me.

His glacial stare was like a torch to the frozen, icy walls that had been erected around my heart.

"A chance for what?" I whispered, clinging to the cup of yogurt like my life depended on it. What was his endgame here? I knew he didn't want anything with me; he'd made that abundantly clear when we broke up.

His feet shuffled until his warm fingers were gently grasping the yogurt. The air sparked like a live wire between us.

"A chance to fix it all, Kat. I want you back."

And there it was—a truth, another confession I wasn't ready for. My heart, however, acted as if I'd just plunged a needle full of adrenaline into it. The erratic beat pounded painfully behind my chest as I processed his words. His fingers began to unfurl, sliding slowly down my arm until they were cupping my elbow.

I blinked, pushing away images of that drunken night when he had me laid down in front of him, his tongue tracing a path to my inner thigh, his own whispered confessions spoken into my skin.

"Do you even remember what you did?" I sidestepped him, needing the distance to remind me of what exactly was going on here, what he was doing, and—more importantly—what he was capable of.

"Do I remember?" His scoff unsettled me. "How could I forget?"

He turned away from me, his body heat leaving me so fast it felt like opening a window in the dead of winter.

"I have to live with what I did to you, Kat. Why do you think I'm here, trying to fix it?"

"Yet, you can't even say it out loud," I argued back, stepping toward him with renewed fire.

He ran his fingers through his hair. "What do you want me to say? That I humiliated you in front of all our friends?"

It was my turn to scoff. "Our friends? Try everyone we have ever known! My father and all of his associates were there, your father's, people I was going to try to intern with—I was supposed to go to law school, and you blacklisted me!" I yelled, pointing a defensive finger at my chest. "You ruined any chance I had at finding future employment. I ended up as a fucking legal aid, an assistant, and now"—I took a step closer, feeling emboldened—"I'm the laughingstock of the evening news thanks to your vet bit."

Shame settled inside my gut, hard and painful. I turned away from him, too humiliated to relive the past.

"You shattered me. Back then, it wasn't even about the connections I lost, the attorneys and partners who saw me as a desperate gold digger, willing to get into anyone's bed for a position. What hurt worse was that I loved you. I was so embarrassingly in love with you, Greyson. So, when you showed up with Tessa—"

"Don't. Just...stop." A large vein protruded from his forehead.

I stepped closer, aligning our heaving chests. "When I saw the engagement ring on her finger instead of mine, my heart physically hurt. I vomited in the bathroom before I went home. I didn't leave my bed for days, because the boy I loved more than anything had tricked me. Everyone knew it was a lie, knew you were only with me as a joke."

"It was never a joke." Greyson's eyes flashed with anger and regret. "We were never a joke." He pointed a finger at his own chest.

I swallowed the thick lump of hurt that had lodged itself in my throat. It had been years; I was past this.

I stepped back. "It's fine, it's been forever, I'm over it. Just don't talk about getting chances or act like you want me and we'll be fine."

"Kat…" His whisper was so soft, so broken it nearly shattered whatever was still standing inside me.

"Please, Greyson." I closed my eyes, trying to push back the rhythm of tears that begged to be released.

"I know I made some mistakes, but please…just give me a chance."

I didn't realize he'd stepped close enough to grip my wrist. It caused an inferno to stretch across my skin, as if he'd taken a real flame to my skin and burned it.

I had to reach for something…anything, self-preservation kicking in. "It wouldn't matter anyway…even if I wanted to give you a chance, I'm seeing someone, remember?"

I stepped back, blinked, and tried to decipher the look on his face.

Dread…anger…then sadness, all crossing his features within seconds, as if he'd been waiting for some truth to fall between us like a wall, permanently dividing us from one another.

"Right." He took a step back, then another…then a few more, his body heat retreating and then completely gone with the tiny click of the front door.

I waited a few pointless seconds, as though he'd come back in and obliterate the wall I'd just shoved between us...but he didn't. I softly walked to the door and locked it.

Four years earlier

"Wear this one tonight." Selah walked over with a white dress bag hanging over her arm. I was so giddy I didn't even care that the dress was borrowed from one of my sister's fancy clients. She was interning with some posh designer like in *The Devil Wears Prada*, except her boss was magnificent and always let her borrow things. I was usually uncomfortable with it, but not tonight.

I carefully pulled the dress free and marveled at how beautiful the buttery fabric was. It was a deep purple, and utterly perfect. I looked up, beaming at my sister.

"It's perfect!"

"Greyson is going to freak out when he sees you in this, and my God, your engagement photos are going to be so perfect!"

We both jumped excitedly together. Tonight was the night Greyson was going to propose. He had been dropping hints for the past week, and I'd even felt him measure my ring finger when he thought I was asleep. We'd been dating for the past year, and I knew it would happen tonight, during our big night. We'd made it through freshman year at Berkeley, and tonight, the Knox Law Firm and its partners—including my father's company, Thomas Structural—would be there together for the first time in twenty years.

An intense feud had brewed between the Knox family and ours for generations. Someone had let it slip once that it had to do with a Knox proposing to a girl, only to have her run away with a Thomas. The two eventually married and produced heirs…all the way down to my father…down to me. That war merged with their corporate relations, and on and on they went, hating one another.

Selah had a theory that Mr. Knox hated our father with a fury like no other because his own wife had left him for another man—a destitute man, saying love was worth living for, not money. She'd fought for custody of her son, Greyson, but from what Selah had learned, she'd lost and was not able to fight the dirty legal tricks her husband had pulled. Greyson experienced ten years of kindness from Hillary, ten years of sunshine and smiles, of happiness and joy. That was it. After she lost custody, she disappeared from his life for good.

I wasn't sure if it was true or not, because my father, even with his faults, was a softer man, and from what I knew of him, he would have shown kindness toward the younger Knox after learning that his mother had been ripped from his life. *Right?* But when my father had first learned I was dating Greyson Knox, he'd nearly disowned me, said it was the biggest mistake of my life. Still, Greyson wore him down. Family dinners, game nights, and with Selah talking him up, it was all finally going to pay off.

Greyson was going to announce that we were together in the most unforgettable way imaginable.

Marriage.

Finally mending the rift between our families once and for all.

Once I was dressed and ready for the party, I sipped champagne until it was time to head into the massive ballroom where our class had gathered. Vanessa, one of my friends from school, met me, smothering a smile, sipping on her own champagne.

It was a networking meeting, but it was also a night Greyson had said would be big for us. We'd show our hopeful mentors and future employers who we were, shake their hands, get our names on lists for future opportunities.

It was supposed to start at seven sharp. The servers were there, filling drinks. Hors d'oeuvres were out and a few people were milling around, but Greyson hadn't shown yet.

I checked my phone: no messages, no anything from him since earlier that morning, when he'd told me he loved me and he couldn't wait for tonight. Worry started to gnaw at my stomach, and I grabbed it on instinct.

Vanessa was still talking about what she'd done over the weekend, oblivious to what was happening in the room. There were murmurs, whispers, which was how I first knew something was off.

I looked around, seeing my father walk through a side door, a few of his associates accompanying him. My stomach tightened for a new reason.

My father and I had a strained relationship, not just because of Greyson, but because he'd divorced my mother when I was twelve and only managed to see Selah and me when it fit into his corporate schedule. Even after our mother died two years later, he had nannies and hired people to take care of us. He doted on us with money and cars as we grew up, made sure we went to the right schools and met the right people. We were in the right social circles for him to be proud, but he was always emotionally distant.

He saw me and tipped his head as though I were someone he'd met a long time ago and he was just trying to be courteous. *Nice.*

It wasn't that I thought he'd be proud of me for getting married to a Knox; it was more like I wanted him to know I just didn't give a damn what he thought either way.

I sipped more champagne as I watched my father talk to his friends, and they all looked around as if they were being inconvenienced to be there. It wasn't even us who had gotten them to arrive—it was this merger they'd announced between Knox Industries. Greyson's family was obnoxious enough to have numerous multibillion-dollar companies.

Minutes ticked by. Still no Greyson, or Mr. Knox. Still no answer to my text messages, asking why my boyfriend was running thirty minutes behind. More and more students were showing up, some not in any of our law classes, some I hadn't seen at any of our parties over the year.

Our obnoxious, elitist parties included the same people, the richest families in California all snorting, drinking, and fucking away all the problems their families' wealth had created. My sister and I went to a few, but then we stopped because our people were the ones who did 7-Eleven runs for spiked Slurpees at midnight and wanted to challenge each other to a killer beats session on the VR while drunk.

Totino's pizzas, cheap vodka, trashy music—those were our people, but once I started dating Greyson, I started hanging with his friends. His friends were pricks.

But, oddly, none of them were present…

What the hell was going on?

Suddenly the music stopped, people stopped talking, and everyone's gaze cut toward the double doors near the fountain.

Mr. Knox walked in, three men flanking him; his eyes cut toward me in an angry way. I had the distinct impression that if he could shoot lasers from those watery grey globes, he'd kill me on the spot.

I watched as he looked around, a grim look on his face as he trudged toward my father. They shared only a few tense nods and what looked like angry words before another set of doors opened. I saw his tousled blond hair first, the way it was skewed across his tan forehead in a manner that screamed playboy.

I smiled and started for him, a small crowd coming with him, pouring into the room, laughter and hollers echoing around the space. I forgot about Vanessa as I cut through small groups and around tables.

He was here. It was happening. But as I drew closer, it was the strangest thing. It was like time had stopped, and I'd somehow traveled into another dimension, like in that *Stranger Things* show...I was there but not there. I could see everyone, hear them, but my breathing had turned ragged, stifled inside my chest.

Because Greyson wasn't alone. He had Tessa on his arm—no, not just on his arm. His hand was around her waist, their fingers interconnected, her bright smile mixing with her caramel skin, making her look like a fucking Egyptian princess.

Greyson's head was ducked down, his smile wide as his friends laughed around him.

I cut my gaze toward my father, wondering if this was all some big joke…but he was only staring at Greyson with confusion and a little bit of rage.

What the hell is going on?

Mr. Knox grabbed a microphone that had been set up for the evening. I assumed there would be speeches and possibly jokes made to entertain everyone.

"Thank you all for coming tonight. We're very excited about the big news we have to break to everyone and what kind of future job opportunities this will create for you as you continue with your college years."

My father whispered to someone next to him, who put a finger in his ear, talking into his wrist. I resisted the urge to roll my eyes—had he really brought a security team with him? I guess it sort of made sense; he'd been in a feud with Knox for over twenty years.

I pushed forward, trying to get closer to Greyson, still confused about what in the world was going on. Maybe Tessa was his cousin or a family friend and they were just being…

My thoughts cut off along with my steps as Greyson planted a searing kiss on Tessa's mouth.

Never fucking mind.

Anger ripped through me as I stood there like an idiot watching as the man I loved kissed someone else.

His father started talking again.

"To kick off the evening, how about some good news? My son, Greyson, has just announced his engagement to Tessa James. A smart match, and a truly exciting partnership." He began clapping, along with everyone in the room—everyone but me.

Greyson kept his head down, his hand clamped tight on Tessa's, her other hand out, showcasing a massive diamond.

The survivor inside me told me to tuck tail and run away, sort this shit out later, not in front of everyone, but damn. Damn him and everyone here. Just the night before he'd fucked me, told me he loved me. Just the night before it had been me he'd held in his arms.

Hurt and outraged, I walked forward, edging around crowds of people who were now congratulating each other. I needed to get to him, except now it was a different voice ringing out of the speakers throughout the room.

"Is this some kind of joke?" my father asked, booming loud and angry. Shit was about to get very real, very fast.

Mr. Knox lazily swung his gaze to my father and bellowed loud enough for all to hear. "Not at all."

"I was told it was Greyson and my daughter Kelly who were getting engaged," my father stated coldly. He'd known Greyson was going to propose? I had thought he'd planned a separate partnership with Knox all on his own, apart from me.

I looked at the expressions around the room as people ducked their heads, guilty as ever. Of course they were, because they'd seen Greyson and me together all year. All fucking year we'd been a couple—why would Greyson think that could just be erased in mere moments?

Greyson shuffled to the right, making his way around the group of people, to where my father stood. Tessa was still attached to him, like a fucking stage five clinger.

He patted my father on the arm like they were old pals then took the microphone.

Everyone huddled closer, like they'd been waiting for him to speak, like he was the main attraction of the night.

"Let me clear the air: yes, it's true I dated Kelly Thomas for part of the year, but more recently, her motives for dating me were uncovered." He darted his eyes toward my father, now with obvious mirth. "It will never be tolerated in the Knox family for anyone to be there merely for selfish gain. When Ms. Thomas heard what a marriage could do for her father's company, she jumped at the chance. Unfortunately, she's no stranger to warming the right person's bed to get ahead or procure a small financial tip for her father's company." His eyes moved like a laser, dead set on finishing me off. His gaze turned into something angry and vicious as he sneered, "You just couldn't refuse, could you?"

What. The. Actual…

"You little fucking liar!" my father roared, ready to lash out at Greyson, but several men in black suits were already there restraining him.

My heart beat erratically within my chest.

This isn't real.

This isn't happening.

What is he talking about? What has he been told, and who told him? I had to get to him.

"I have proof of her plans, of her other lovers." His eyes cut down the middle of the room, right to where I stood. Hate was obvious and clearly written all over his face.

It nearly stole the air right out of my lungs.

"I'm so glad you're all here to witness this, because in order to enforce this, we'll need help. Kelly Thomas is hereby blacklisted from Berkeley. She's not to set foot on this side of fucking town again, and if I find out you've helped her, befriended her, or invited her to a party, you're blacklisted too. Check who cuts those big checks to Berkeley if you're tempted to try me."

Wave after wave of anger mixed with hurt hit me in the chest, like it was vibrating right off him. If he would just let me explain or tell my side of this...although, what *side*? This whole entire thing was bullshit.

Every eye in the place turned toward me, looking on with disgust.

I tried to say something, anything, but there was a thick lump of pain caught in my throat. If I opened my mouth, a sob would come out, and I did not—would not sob in front of this crowd. I wouldn't shed a fucking tear.

If he wanted to do this, we would do it. I saw security coming toward me; I lifted my chin and stared at Greyson, shaking my head, then walked away.

If he wanted to be done, we'd be fucking finished forever.

8

KELLY

"Good morning, boss!" Payton said in a happy, singsong voice. She was too chipper for eight in the morning. I had never been allowed to be that chipper for Aubrey when I was her assistant. She wasn't rude about it, but we both mutually agreed it was just unacceptable to be perky or happy until well after nine AM. I sighed wistfully, thinking back to my life when I was the assistant at a law firm.

I wore cute clothes, and I worked for one of my favorite people in the whole world. Aubrey would trade off days with me on who got who lunch and coffee. I would take the odd days, because I wanted to be a good assistant, but she always fought me on it, making Friday our even day where she'd buy lunch and I'd buy coffee.

Thinking about my old boss and friend made an ache begin to grow inside me, splintering like an old piece of wood. I missed my old life, but more than that, I missed Aubrey. I missed calling her and doing yoga with her, but damn, I was happy for her. I was so happy she'd found Chance, but I still missed her.

Remembering that I was being strangely quiet, I smiled at Payton and replied, "Morning."

I needed coffee, which reminded me...

I pushed into my office, set my things down, and called the flower shop. I needed to make it look like I had a doting boyfriend who sent me beautiful flowers while I was at work. It was a tad pathetic, but the memory of Greyson's eyes from the night before made me feel better about it.

I had wrestled all night with what had transpired between us, how his eyes had spoken a thousand apologies, declaring a truth he hadn't told me all those years ago. These were thoughts I hadn't allowed myself to entertain when I was alone and brokenhearted, but I had wondered if there was more to the story when he blindsided me with that engagement, one that ended shortly after I tucked tail and ran away.

I turned my computer monitor on, moving the mouse, trying to work so I wouldn't focus on all the little details that had acted like small arrows, piercing me and flaying me open. He'd hurt me so badly back then, but...

There was so much that didn't make any sense. The way his angry glare caught on mine but flashed back toward his father...the way he didn't look at his fiancée. The way he looked like he wanted to drag me down the hall and fix whatever happened between us with our usual toxic chaos of desperate kisses. He had a thousand questions that day—I could see it in his eyes—but he wouldn't ask any of them.

A soft knock on my door tore me from my thoughts. "Come on in," I yelled, typing in my password, pulling up my email and agenda for the day.

"Oh my god! Someone delivered these for you, Kel," Payton gushed, holding a massive bouquet of red roses.

I smiled, wishing we had more of an audience. "Thanks, Payton." I stood to grab the glass vase from her. I needed to scale back a bit. At this rate, if I spent forty dollars on each of my fake boyfriend flower arrangements, I was going to go broke.

I set the vase on my desk and made a show of reading the card right as Julie and Greyson walked in: *"Thanks for last night. Can't wait to see you again."*

"Awww, omg, I love romance, and that card was so sweet!" Payton murmured, bringing her hands to her chest.

Julie walked toward the desk, bent, and inhaled the flowers. Suddenly I felt like shit, thinking maybe I should have just sent them to her. She deserved them; I did not.

"Wow...quite the arrangement," Greyson muttered, keeping one hand in his pocket, the other brushing against a petal. Payton heard the front desk phone ring, forcing her to run out of my office, and Julie received an incoming notification on her phone that had her telling me she'd be right back before she dashed away.

Greyson stood stoically near my desk, staring down at the flowers, and I felt awkward. What was I supposed to do now? Ask him to leave? That seemed aggressive...

"Interesting card..." His tone was accusatory, which immediately made me irritated.

"What is that supposed to mean?" I hated myself for it, but I placed my hand on my hip in a defensive gesture.

"It's just..." He shrugged, his tailored black blazer barely moving out of place. "Must be a brand-new thing...this relationship you have." He carefully moved around the desk, not on my side, just strategically enough to get closer while both his hands disappeared into his pockets.

"Wha-what do you mean?" *Fuck, I stuttered.* Rule number one: never show a sign of weakness in front of a man like Greyson Knox.

I straightened my spine, trying to cover for my mishap.

Greyson stepped to the right, glancing down at his shoes as he talked. "It's just that a comment like thanking you for the night prior—which ended pathetically early for him, by the way—it screams brand new, maybe even a first or second date."

"So what if it was?" I dared to ask.

Greyson made a sound with his lips, forcing my gaze to go there. His eyes were on me, like harsh blue stone, freezing me in place. He leaned against my desk and, in an instant, scooted along it until he was directly in front of me.

"The thing about new relationships, first dates, second dates... they're so fragile. They can snap in half just like *that.*" He snapped his fingers, the sound nearly making me jump.

"Well, I hate to burst your bubble, but it's more serious than that." I huffed, crossing my arms.

Greyson leaned forward, just a little, but it was enough to see the gold specks in his eyes, the only part that looked green... the part you were only able to see if you got close enough.

"If that were true...then..." He trailed off, his eyes still hard on mine, heat simmering inside them, melting me. I was waiting for his next words when I felt a tug on the bow that tied

71

my top together. It only left a bit of the top of my chest on display, the buttons under it keeping the rest of my shirt closed, but it still felt like he'd just stripped me.

"Then what?" I whispered, leaning closer, forgetting myself... the last few years...everything. Damn him. I needed to know what he was going to say, and I needed his hands on my body.

"Then..." he started again, but now he was pulling on the ends of the bow he'd untied, dragging me closer to him.

I wanted to let him pull me closer, wanted to fall into his arms and let his lips land on mine...I wanted to just give in to it and flip my heart the middle finger. It was doing a lousy job lately anyway.

But...

"Then what?" I said again, putting my hands over his, stopping the momentum of my face getting closer to his.

He scanned my face. Clearing his throat, he stood, forcing me to fall back into my computer chair. He was leaning over me in seconds, his lips at my ear, his hot breath fanning my skin as he said, "Then you wouldn't have allowed me to nearly undress you, or almost kiss you. I look forward to seeing if this guy is *really* serious or not."

Ass.

He stood, fixing his suit jacket, then started walking back toward the door, but before he got there, he looked over his shoulder. Smirking he said, "Oh, and Kat, I hate that shirt. I would hate it if you kept wearing shirts like it." He flicked his gaze to my chest before walking out of my office.

I slouched back in my chair and let out a steady breath, wondering how I'd let my guard down so easily. He'd known I would, too, which was exactly why I was so insanely screwed.

The next few days went by devastatingly slowly.

Each day, I would call the garage that had my car, and each day, they'd tell me about another issue they'd found, which meant each day the price to get it working properly was getting higher and higher. One of the most painful things about taking this gig at a nonprofit shelter was the horrific pay cut.

Aubrey and Chance had done all they could to get me a somewhat agreeable salary, but Aubrey knew it was nothing compared to my old wage as her assistant. Since I had been required to also work as a legal aid, my salary had been set a bit higher when I was hired with Sherman, Kline, and Lefave LLP.

But, when Aubrey moved away, she'd inspired me with her work at the shelter in Hermosa Beach. She'd taken a massive pay cut, even more so than me, and I wasn't too big of a person to live off my savings for a while. Unfortunately, three stints of my car being at the mechanic had already cut into them pretty horrifically.

At this point, I was about ready to tell them not to worry about the car; they could just keep the damn thing.

Sunlight poured into the play yard, reflecting off the metallic siding on the fences. The sounds of happy barks and playful yips surrounded me as I went to one knee and embraced the black bundle of sleek fur that pummeled toward me.

"Jet, baby boy, how are you?" I patted his belly playfully. I was in a pair of cute skinny jeans and a loose V-neck t-shirt, trying to stay comfortable enough to sneak out and walk my favorite guy. I needed time away from the shelter, and while I had been doing a lot of my work at night while at home, I didn't want to exactly broadcast that I was trying not to be in the shelter as much as possible. Even so, I was fairly sure my assistant already knew.

"Wanna go for a walk?" I let him kiss my face, like a total sucker. Never in a million years would I let a dog slide his tongue across my face, but I was a goner for Jet.

I snapped a leash to his plain green collar and smiled at a few volunteers who were also headed into the play area to walk a few of the dogs. I knew they were probably confused as to why I kept coming in to see Jet, why I insisted on being the one to feed him every morning and evening, and why I wanted to be the one to walk him.

This thing between us was getting worse, and I was about ready to give up my apartment just to have Jet. Smiling, I ventured toward Slater Park, where many of our dog walkers usually went.

I walked slowly, not in any rush or hurry to get back.

"Wanna share an ice cream cone?" I knelt down and rubbed Jet's fur, and without knowing why or what was coming over me, I leaned in closer until I was hugging him. I held on tight, feeling a surge of emotion hit me in the chest.

The last week hung heavy over my head as memories banged hard against my mind, reminding me of all the hurts I'd buried and never faced.

Tears streamed down my face as I hugged Jet. I clung to him, hearing his breathing, feeling his drool on my arms. God, I was a mess, but I knew deep down that the breakdown was overdue and I just needed to let it happen.

Once I was finished, I wiped my face and laughed at how strange it felt to have an animal to confide in, to take shelter in. It was the weirdest sensation I'd ever felt, this love that had overwhelmed me from the inside out. I wasn't ready for it.

But it made me feel less broken, knowing I could love again. I could even have a companion. Something I honestly had slightly given up on—now it was there, like a tiny flame, offering me a second chance, a fresh start without romance… without Greyson fucking Knox.

"Did you see your calendar?" Julie asked while picking at her Caesar salad. I sipped my soda and tried to answer without an immature sigh. I hadn't exactly been thrilled to check my calendar now that Greyson had started scheduling me for things.

"I glanced at it briefly today…" I trailed off, letting her draw whatever conclusions she wanted to draw.

Julie stopped chewing. "Seriously?"

"What?" I asked, returning her raised brow. I didn't want to know how many times a day I would be forced to see Greyson. I focused on budgets, balancing the forecasted few months, summer events, what we were going to do for Christmas, and a few other things that needed planned out when I wasn't avoiding the shelter.

Anything to keep me from potentially running into him.

"Kelly, you're going to be hosting a pet adoption with him this afternoon in the park!" she shrieked, clambering for her cell phone.

I let out a sigh. One guess as to who thought that one up.

"Greyson planned it?" I asked, shoving a few more bites of taco salad in my mouth.

"Nope, this one was all Chance. He called this morning and I tried to call you, but you were out of the office...or at least that's what your calendar said."

Oh shit.

I stood quickly, making our lunch table shake. We were outside, a few blocks down from the shelter, taking in the sun and the iced lattes a small food truck was serving.

"I was at the mechanic, trying to see if I could get my car back." I started picking up my plastic fork and napkins. Stupid car and stupid diagnosis; the starter is out, the brakes are shot, the steering column is jacked up. Blah, blah, give us a thousand dollars and we'll start working it in—but that doesn't include the cost of parts. Bottom line, I still had no car, and I was no closer to keeping my savings intact.

"What time this afternoon?" I didn't have the right outfit on for a pet adoption. I was in sleek slacks, high heels, and a pressed, flowy blouse that couldn't get hair all over it—unless it was Jet's. I didn't care about getting his hair on me.

Panic blossomed through each thought as I started tossing my lunch away. Why on earth had Chance arranged this? He never arranged anything with the shelter, although I knew he was a big part of why Aubrey had wanted to keep it going after the partners left.

Julie checked her watch, chucking her lunch as I'd done with mine. "You have an hour."

"We haven't even advertised the event…this is so out of left field, why on earth…" I trailed off, trying to rack my brain for what Chance was possibly thinking.

"He said something about an organic, authentic vibe…basically we're going to set up then have Greyson there to take pictures and do free, informative pet care demonstrations and whatever else," Julie explained, waving her hand around, dismissing my panic.

"Okay…why do I need to be there? I mean, I can be there as a support member, but why not have a few volunteers out there with Greyson?" I shrugged, walking down the street toward the shelter.

"Chance said he and Aubrey want to keep building on the shelter momentum. Greyson is paying for this crew to keep getting coverage for the shelter's YouTube channel, but they need events to actually film, and since you've been pretty scarce these last few days, I guess Greyson pitched the idea to Chance through email…"

We power-walked down a few more blocks, ignoring how the sun was peeking in and out of a massive grey sky. Today wasn't the best day to do this pet adoption idea. Why on earth rush it? Why not let us plan one and have it on a day when it wasn't going to pour outside?

"Anyway, I guess Greyson mentioned that he thought the subscribers would want you both there…" Julie trailed off again, her breaths coming in and out a little harsher now. We were walking pretty fast, so I slowed a bit.

Scrunching my nose, I turned toward her. "But…"

She put up a hand. "Do you even know what they're saying? You and Greyson are a huge hit. We have almost ten thousand subscribers, which is insane for a nonprofit animal shelter in Temecula," Julie explained in a rush. "They love you guys—look at the comments!" She shoved her phone in my face, where I saw comment after comment mentioning Greyson and me. "They created a hashtag for you guys: #greyskat..." Julie's brown eyes softened.

"Come on," I scoffed, "you aren't one of them, are you?" I handed her phone back.

"Look, I get that you're new to the nonprofit world, but donations are a big thing. The more we get, the more animals we can help, the more youth outreach projects we can sponsor... we won't exist without donors."

Now my stupid heart softened. "Julie, I want to do everything I can to help get us the money we need, but I won't pretend there's something there with Greyson when there's not."

Julie's lips pinched together, making her seem contemplative. She paused for a moment before squinting at the low-hanging clouds. "But...would you really be pretending? Everyone can see there's something between you two. I mean, you should see the way he looks at you when you don't know he's watching. Like when you go see Jet—I saw him leaning against the wall the other day, watching you with this huge smile on his face."

I winced as an unexpected feeling of hurt and worry slammed into me. No, this was a game to Greyson, nothing more.

"Sorry, that was out of line...I shouldn't have said that..." Julie caught up with me as I began walking again.

"It's fine, Julie, really. There's just a lot of water under that bridge."

"Look, don't pretend or embellish anything. Just show up, smile, and be yourself, okay? That's all Chance wants. He never mentioned anything about faking or making anything seem like it was more, and you know Aubrey wouldn't ever agree with that anyway."

I nodded my head, knowing that was true. Aubrey would never in a million years try to make this seem like it was more than what it was. She and Chance were likely just picking up on the opportunity to have free camera footage of shelter events.

"I'll be there with bells on." I smiled and turned for the front door.

9

KELLY

THE SUN PARTED the gloomy sky, making the grass look greener and the puppies look sweeter. There were kittens, adult cats, and a few adult dogs too, all within a few different pens.

There were at least twenty people milling about, holding fuzzy balls of cuteness, and getting kisses from the sweetest dogs in the shelter. My heart beat hard with hope for these animals. I wanted them cared for, taken home. Although we cared for them well, it was still a temporary space for them. We were a no-kill shelter, so some of our pets had been there longer, but we worked hard to ensure we found homes for every creature that came through our doors.

I walked over and held in a tiny breath as I saw which dogs they'd brought to the fair. My eyes scanned each cage, praying selfishly that he hadn't been brought today. Just as I was about to let out a sigh of relief, a flash of black caught my eye.

Jet was set up in one of the pens with a little girl bent low, patting his head. Pain and panic squeezed my chest. *No.*

I stepped forward on instinct, like my feet would automatically carry me to him.

I didn't want to lose him. The small, teeny-tiny part of me that wasn't selfish knew this was good for him; he needed a good home, so maybe this was for the best.

I felt eyes on me as I watched the little girl giggle while Jet licked her face. He was gentle, always gentle.

"That bother you?" Greyson asked, coming up from behind me. We'd managed to avoid each other for the first hour of the adoption fair, but now his husky voice was like a slow, tantalizing burn down my back.

"No, why would it?" I lied, not turning to see that shade of blue I was starting to love again.

"Because you love that dog. Do you always give up what you love so easily?"

The little girl was showing her mother, waving her hand expressively toward Jet. He'd be adopted within the hour and I'd never see him again.

I turned away from the scene and faced Greyson. "I only give up on things I know could or should never be mine."

I gave him a pointed look and walked away.

A second later, he was on my heels, his zesty cologne wrapping around me.

"Kat," he hissed as we walked past a few volunteers with clipboards. We all wore matching sky blue shirts that said Park Street Animal Shelter, and it was a nice way to blend in.

I didn't want to talk, not when my heart felt like it was in my throat over losing Jet. I knew he'd be gone after today, and I'd never have him to talk to again, never have his soft fur to soothe me when the pain of being alone got to be too much.

"Kat!" Greyson gently tugged on my elbow, stopping me. We were in public, and people were watching. At least with the shirts, people wouldn't be able to specifically identify Greyson or myself so easily.

"Stop it, Greyson. Stop talking to me about things you have no business talking to me about." I tugged my elbow back, but he just used the movement as a way to get me closer.

He turned us and planted my back against a tree, his arm going up to shield our faces. His lips were close to mine, so dangerously close as he leaned in to whisper, "I know you. I know you wanted that dog—why didn't you just adopt him?"

I searched his eyes. They were soft, worried...searching for something deeper. I knew he was talking about more than just the dog.

I licked my dry lips, and he tracked the movement, getting closer. I could feel his firm chest against mine, and it was like we'd gone back in time.

"I'll love you forever, even when we end...even when it's over...even then, I'm yours."

It was what he'd whispered into my ear one night when he thought I was asleep. I felt cold metal against my finger that night...a ring. He'd placed a ring on my finger, but when I woke, there was nothing there.

I needed to stop thinking of how we'd been then and focus on what I was striving for now.

"My apartment won't allow pets." I looked down, wishing this seemingly intimate moment would end.

"Then move," his husky voice grated along my neck, his lips branding the skin next to my ear.

I shook my head, feeling tears begin. "It's not that simple…"

He forced my chin up. "It is. If you want something, just take it."

His eyes were pinned to my lips, his words soft but firm, so full of guilt and hope…an odd mixture that wormed its way through me.

He was challenging me again, and it lit a fire in me, something so bright and alive. If we had been alone, I'd have kissed him. I wanted to; I missed what it felt like to be in his arms.

Except…I was supposed to have someone…

I blinked, stepping out of his embrace. "I need to go call Gavin."

"Who the fuck is Gavin?" Greyson asked, anger ripping through his tone.

"He's the guy I'm seeing." I tried to walk past him.

"You're really still playing at that?" His fingers wrapped around my wrist in a gentle but firm hold.

"I'm not playing at anything. He's…" I started, but Greyson moved closer, catching me entirely off guard. His hand went to my hip, pushing me back up against the tree. His nose went to my hair, his lips to my ear, carefully skimming the shell of it.

He breathed out. "We both know he's not."

Shit, he knew, and I hadn't even pretended to have a fake boyfriend for very long. Now what was I supposed to do?

"Grey, let me go," I softly requested, my chest rising and falling in a harsh rhythm.

"I did that once, Kat—worst mistake of my life. I'll release my grip, but understand me when I say..." He pressed his fingers more firmly into my hip, his fingers pushing up my shirt. "I'm not done yet."

My heart raced like a stallion, kicking and thrashing to get away from the one man who'd betrayed it so horribly.

He let go an instant later and walked away.

I sucked in a breath, placing a hand on my chest as I headed toward the bathrooms. I needed a second to recover without anyone watching or hovering nearby.

An hour later, we were packing things up, and Jet was gone. I hadn't seen the girl leave with him, but I knew he'd been adopted. I knew I'd never see him again.

Hurt wound around my heart like a thick line of barbed wire, but I pushed past it, packed my things, and readied myself for the bus.

I stood with my hoodie zipped up, my purse on my shoulder as the rest of the volunteers headed back to the shelter with the cages, carriers, and tables tucked into the trunks of their func-tional vehicles. I had lost track of Greyson after our little chat, which was good because everyone seemed to be buzzing about us. I'd heard our name whispered a few times as I passed by groups and as I watched him do a demonstration on how to properly cut a dog's nails.

I needed to move on, past the lust that kept filling me up every time he so much as looked in my direction. I needed distance.

As I made my way toward the bus stop, it started raining again, the grey sky firmly back in place after a few good hours of sunshine.

I was regretting not bringing my umbrella when I heard my name being called. I turned around, blinking at the fat rain-drops falling against my face.

Greyson was pulling up to the curb, in the spot where the bus would be pulling up any second. His dark Range Rover glistened in the rain as he leaned over the console, trying to get my attention.

"Kat, get in the car!" he yelled again. The other bus riders did a double take at us both, a few looking down the main artery of the street to see if the bus was coming. Greyson was going to clog the system if he didn't move his car.

"Greyson, move! Get out of here—I'm taking the bus!" I yelled back, not moving toward his car a single inch.

"I'm not moving until you get in the car!" he called back, putting his vehicle into park.

A few seconds blinked by, him staring at me, me staring at him. I was freezing, rain soaking my clothes, but I was also blistering hot from the way his stare burned through me.

He watched me as water splashed in through his open passenger window, marring the leather interior.

A few people milling around the bus stop cleared their throats as we engaged in our stare-down. One person yelled something about taking him up on his offer if I didn't jump in. I ignored them, like I ignored him. The rain increased its angry tempo, slapping against the concrete, forcing me to put my purse up over my head.

"Kat, get in the fucking car before I come out there and get you!" Greyson repeated.

He was going to delay the bus, which would mess with everyone's schedules, and some people were getting to their second job. I saw a few panicked glances from around the group and then peeked down the road. Sure enough, the top of the bus was in view from the road, heading right for us.

"Fine! Oh my gosh, I'm getting in."

I climbed into his fancy car, sopping wet, and shut the door, praying the bus wouldn't have any issue with picking up the passengers.

As the window closed and Greyson pulled away from the curb, the warmth from the air vents settled around me. My butt was starting to feel warm too with the dual seat warmers on. I relaxed into the seat as he started down the street, not heading toward my side of town.

"Where are we going?" I asked the windshield, refusing to look at him.

"I'm feeding you, then I'll take you home," Greyson replied gruffly.

Desperate to stick to my fake story, I cleared my throat. "I'm sure Gavin will come by later with food, so you can just take me home."

He laughed. The asshole actually laughed.

"Gavin...yes, I'd love to meet the guy you're seeing, the one who just happened to let you ride the bus in a massive downpour. He does know the bus stop where you get dropped off is half a mile from your apartment, right?"

Damn him.

"He's working. He offered to grab me later, but I didn't want to wait," I replied easily, as if I wasn't totally full of shit.

"Where does he work?"

I eyed Greyson for a second, wondering how many more questions he had loaded.

"Uh...finance. There's a finance building on the other side of town..." *Shit. Double shit.* I forgot that Greyson's entire family worked in finance.

"Interesting, then I would know him—what branch does he work in?" I saw the smallest smirk appear on his face.

"Investments," I mumbled, digging through my purse, trying to play it off.

"What side of town does he live on?" Greyson shot off like a cannon.

"West side." *Shit...wait...*

"So, we're close to where he lives then, and it's past five. I happen to know investment brokers shut down before five...so he should be home, right?"

"Well, he could be at the grocery store," I shot back, desperate to make the lie stick.

"Great, why don't we try to surprise him with takeout? Let's swing by, grab some Chinese, and then you can introduce me to him."

"I would, but I'd be too worried about your safety. He knows about our past and isn't your biggest fan."

Suddenly Greyson deflated, and I was so surprised by the action that I looked over at him. His lips were firmly pressed together into a fine line, his hands clenching the steering wheel. He wasn't happy, but I wasn't about to apologize.

"Just take me home, Grey, please." I softly sighed, sagging against the window.

He put his blinker on, turning onto Fifth Street, slowly veering us toward my side of town.

Relief and remorse swept through me. This was better; we needed space.

Once outside my building, Greyson parked and began to unbuckle...which meant he was walking me up.

Great.

We silently made our way up in the elevator, and Greyson guided me to my door by the small of my back, until I was grabbing my keys and watching our feet.

"Thank you for the ride," I muttered uselessly.

"Kat..." He breathed my name like it was a prayer, like it was his last hope.

He pulled my chin up with his finger, forcing my eyes to shift to him. I couldn't place what the look was, but it was paralyzing.

So much so that when his hand went to my hip, gripping me, I didn't stop his lips from descending.

They were silky against mine, hot and smooth. He gave me no warning before his tongue darted out, tasting me—then it turned vicious. His hand went to the base of my neck, his body pressed into mine as he pushed me against the door, and his other hand went to my thigh, where he pulled it up and wrapped my leg around his waist.

His erection pressed into my core, forcing a riot of molten need to erupt, and of my own accord, I began writhing against him. He bit my lip, reminding me of what we used to be like together, how hard and rough we were with each other. I'd never been like that with anyone after him.

Hot spikes of desire began to unfurl within me, making me whimper with want.

"Dammit, Kat. You're still so fucking perfect," he grated against my neck as he began sucking and kissing, just like I used to love.

"Kiss me again," I begged earnestly. I was so pathetic.

His lips landed on mine, hard and demanding, and the hand on my thigh moved higher, until he was squeezing my ass through my jeans.

I needed him closer.

I rocked my hips forward, desperate for friction of some kind, and he met my thrust with one of his own.

"Take me inside," he said, rough and heavy against my skin.

God, I wanted to.

I needed to.

But...

Damn it all.

"I don't think that's a good idea," I replied, internally berating myself for missing out on the orgasms I knew Greyson would deliver if I did let him inside.

He stepped back, his chest heaving and eyes blazing. It was nearly enough to convince me to let him in, but those tiny tendrils of the past still wrapped around my heart, squeezing tight whenever I thought of that day when he walked in with Tessa. It still hurt. I hadn't moved on or recovered from it, and that was what had me putting on the brakes.

"Gavin?" Greyson asked, taking my hands in his, keeping his gaze there instead of my eyes.

My throat was dry as I lied to him. "Yes."

"Right…" he replied, nodding his head. He knew I was lying, and the fact that he wasn't pushing it too much made my heart flutter with hope.

I turned toward my door as he slid his hands into his slacks, keeping his head lowered.

Questions burned inside my throat, begging for some explanation. For years, I'd let them go, but…

"The night before that party, you kissed my forehead, told me you loved me…" I turned halfway toward him, hoping my whisper was loud enough for him to hear. "Was there anything from our time together that was real, Grey?"

He stood tall, rigid, his hands still shoved into his pockets. Slowly, I let my eyes meet his.

They shone with a million words, secrets, burdens…his brows drew together as he slowly raised his left hand to trace my bottom lip with his thumb. My breath hitched from how slow and intimate it was.

"Do you remember that time we stayed on the beach?"

I nodded, remembering a weekend full of unhurried kisses, hot sex, and waltzing lazily on the sand, the waves lapping at our toes.

"I told you something that weekend, something I had never told anyone…"

I felt the line form between my brows as I thought over what he was saying. Nothing specific stood out about that weekend, other than the sex and lazy walks.

A moment later, I felt his kiss sear my brow line before he turned to leave.

I opened my apartment door and sagged against it as it clicked shut.

What had he told me? And what did it mean in regard to my question?

10

GREYSON

"Good morning, asshole," my best friend practically sang into my ear.

"Shit, what time is it?" I groaned, turning on my side, placing the phone on speaker so Josh's annoying-as-fuck voice wasn't right up against my head.

"It's seven, and you're in deep shit," Josh replied, huffing like he was still doing his cooldown on the treadmill.

"Why are you calling me?" I sat up in bed, rubbing a hand down my face. Last thing I remembered from the night before was dropping Kat off at her place, getting Chinese, and getting shitfaced at home, trying to drown the way it felt to have her so close one second then gone the next.

"I'm calling you because I thought you should know what popped up on Twitter today from some gossip blog. Danny sent it to me—remember that guy? I hated him," Josh remarked, his disdain obvious.

I assumed he was talking about all the gossip that had started over Kat and me working together. People liked us together and had been sharing the shit out of the videos my team had been posting on the shelter's YouTube channel.

I stood, walking toward my bathroom to take a piss, and then Josh's voice stopped me dead in my tracks.

"It's obviously an old photo, but the fact that Tessa retweeted it makes it seem like you're still a thing," my best friend explained cautiously.

"What?" I headed back toward the phone, grabbing it so fast I nearly fell over.

With Josh still on speaker, I navigated on the screen to see what post he was talking about.

"Just go look at Tessa's Twitter account and you'll see her bull-shit feed."

He was right—there on my ex-fake fiancée's Twitter account were several photos of us together, including a few of her kissing animals, tagging me as her favorite vet.

"What the actual fuck..." I muttered, sitting down on the bed, feeling rage start to climb up the inside of my chest like a damn wildfire.

"Tell me you aren't with her again."

"I'm not!" I yelled at the phone in my hand. My eyes raked anxiously over the pictures of Tessa's puckered pink lips kissing a mirror with the caption *Future animal doctor wifey*.

"I'm so confused..." I ran my hand over my head as my best friend sat silent on the other end. "I haven't spoken to Tessa in over a year. It was at some Christmas function my father host-ed..." I trailed off, still staring at the screen, utterly bewildered.

"Well, my guess is she doesn't love missing out on the limelight you and Kat are suddenly in. You probably haven't seen yet, but *Good Morning America* showed your pig video on their show this morning."

Holy hell.

"Fuck, no. I didn't know that." I stood, suddenly panicked about what Kat would think about this news.

"Well figure it out, brother…don't lose what ground you've gained with Kat over this." My best friend's tone was softer, not as jovial or sarcastic, which made the feeling worming through me even worse.

I had gained basically zero ground with Kat, just a hot-as-fuck kiss and grope session. That was it, and this would put us back to who we were all those years ago…when I broke her trust and her heart all in one swift, vicious moment.

"Have you told her yet, about everything?" Josh asked, likely tracking with my mental spiral.

"I haven't," I said quietly, wishing so badly that I had. Because now…

Fuck.

"Shit, dude. Why not?"

"I was…I don't know, fucking weak, I guess. Now this shit is going to blow up in my face. Why did it have to be Tessa of all women who tried to pull this stunt?"

Josh scoffed, "Man, I don't know, but you need to get to her before anyone else does."

He was right—I had to get to her first. It was early enough, and I might just make it.

I rushed through the doors at a quarter to eight. I'd called Kat's cell number twice with no luck of getting through, and if I tried much more, I worried it would make me seem guilty.

Which I wasn't.

This was all just some bullshit mistake.

Our front desk girl wasn't in yet, which gave me hope that I'd catch Kat in time. If I remembered her routine correctly from when we dated, she wouldn't check the news or her emails until she got into work. She always preferred to start her day by reading her Kindle, saying she would rather begin her morning with a dose of good, getting that smile plastered to her face that she could only get from a good book.

I loved that about her. So defiant, so brilliant. She would have easily passed the bar on her first try, and if I hadn't screwed things up for her, she would have found the best firm to intern with.

I couldn't believe I'd made it where she was just assisting with legal cases and supporting lawyers instead of being the one practicing law. I had done that to her. I'd made it impossible for her to go to law school, unless she wanted to move away— which, knowing how close she was with her sister, I knew she would never do.

I walked toward Kat's office, made sure she wasn't in yet, then headed for my office, back near the dog kennels.

My first order of business would be to contact the blog who'd posted the piece about Tessa and myself and demand they take it down. The next thing I needed to do was get in touch with Tessa and figure out what game she was playing at.

I was in the middle of typing the first email when I heard someone yell from the front of the shelter.

I stood, moving closer so I could see what was going on.

"Grey?!" Kat yelled as she walked farther into the building.

I met her halfway and stopped dead in my tracks when I realized what was in her arms.

"Is that a——?"

"Yes." She had tears welling up in her eyes, and her cute-as-fuck flirty skirt was drenched with little splatters of mud along the edges. Her white shirt and blazer were ruined with mud from the bundle in her arms.

"Where did you find it?" I asked, moving closer.

"I decided to walk to work this morning, and it was lying under this big box, shaking so bad and all messed up." She shuddered while passing the tiny creature to me.

"It's a duck." I marveled, not even sure I knew what it was under all that muck on its feathers.

"Yes, a duck," Kat said, wiping a tear from her face, leaving a trail of dirt.

"I thought it was a kitten," I murmured, still staring down at the strange thing.

"No...a duckling, and we need to help it." She urged me toward the back of the shelter, where the operating room was.

"Of course," I assured her. Just then, I saw the first camera guy showing up for the day. He caught my eye, pulled out his cell, and jogged after us.

"Is it going to live?" Kat asked, her voice tight with worry.

"I won't know until I can get it cleaned up and see what's wrong with it." I shoved through the swinging doors and set the lifeless bird on a stainless-steel table.

"Hang in there, Gus," Kat whispered, trailing her pointer finger down its neck.

"You named it?" I turned the knobs, getting the taps ready for the duck to be washed up.

Kat just nodded then started stripping out of her blazer and rolling her sleeves up.

A moment later, she was next to me, elbow to elbow, helping me wash the duck. Her honeysuckle scent wrapped around me like a comforting hug, silencing all the fears that had started banging against my pathetic heart this morning.

Our fingers brushed up against each other as we gently catered to Gus, and I noticed her lip trembling, which gave me pause. As long as I'd known Kat, she'd never been overly affectionate toward animals. She didn't hate them, but she had planned to be a lawyer, and most of us just didn't have that soft bone, making us vulnerable toward animals, or even nurturing, for that matter.

"Hey, it's going to be okay," I whispered to her, wishing my hands were dry so I could trace a finger down her spine. She used to love when I did that.

She sniffed, shrugging her shoulders. "It's just that it's so little…I want it to make it."

Something deep down told me she wasn't just talking about the bird.

"It will," I said hoarse and full of apology, not taking my eyes off her.

Those blue eyes bounced up to mine, holding while we both had our hands around the duck. Our shoulders were connected, and our chests rose and fell with accelerated breathing.

The blinding light from Damon's camera brought us out of our staring contest, forcing us to break apart.

Once the duck was clean, I laid it out on the table and took a look at its wing.

Kat was leaned over, her head bent close to mine as I examined the tiny animal. I carefully looked over its body, but there didn't seem to be anything wrong with it.

"I think it's just malnourished, but otherwise it'll be okay." I reached over to grab a towel, wrapping it around the impossibly small duckling.

Kat reached forward, grabbing the bundle and pulling it to her chest.

"So, nothing is broken?" She stepped closer to me, reminding me of what had happened between us the previous night. I had assumed she'd be closed off and skittish toward me today, but she seemed more connected than ever.

I stepped closer, arching my neck toward her and Gus, letting her feel the heat of my body next to hers.

"He'll be okay. We'll get a volunteer to set him up with vitamins and get him settled near the pond out back. He'll be right as rain."

Our chests nearly connected, with just the little feathered bundle between us, and I scanned the smattering of freckles that decorated Kat's face, right under her eyes. Her makeup usually hid them, but if you were lucky enough to get a close look, it was like a miniature constellation of stars.

I brought my finger up to her hairline to push back a stray strand. It was two seconds of silky perfection before Kat realized we were being recorded.

She broke contact first, which made me want to put my fist through Damon's camera. I wouldn't do that, or even act like I didn't want the intrusion, because I was doing all this for the shelter. I had personally hired the crew, and I'd had a video call with both Aubrey and Chance to interview for this position, during which I informed them of my charitable ideas to help the shelter get more traffic.

I was doing this for a good cause, and because the woman now attached to running the place held my heart in her dainty hands.

I nodded toward Damon to let him know the segment was over, and it was also our way of communicating without words that I didn't want to be on camera at the moment. Some conversations didn't need an audience.

I followed after Kat, knowing she was headed toward the break area to see if any volunteers were in yet. I already knew we had a few milling around, just from the sounds of lockers slamming shut in the back.

I hung back while Kat handed Gus off to Jennifer, one of our volunteers who had lived on a farm her whole life. She would likely adopt the little thing and make sure it was okay.

After Kat was finished talking with the volunteers and checking in on the projects listed on the white board, I followed her to her office.

"Thank you for your help today," she said as the air left her lungs and she landed hard in her chair. She seemed exhausted, and it wasn't even nine in the morning yet.

"That's why I'm here." I shoved my hands into the pockets of my scrubs and leaned against her wall. Fuck, I didn't want to have this ridiculous conversation. "Kat, I need to tell you something," I started, but just then Julie rushed through the office door, cutting me off.

"Kat, I have some donors up front who'd love to talk with you. Sounds like they've been in touch with Aubrey via email, and she encouraged them to come in this morning to talk with you. I'll be honest…I think you should offer to take them to coffee. We're talking deep pockets here."

Kat blinked then flicked her gaze to mine briefly before nodding her head at Julie.

"Grey, can we talk maybe later today?" she asked, shrugging back into her semi-soiled blazer. She didn't seem to mind that it had little bits of mud on the sleeves or near the collar.

I smiled at her, trying to seem upbeat about the conversation. "Of course."

I mentally begged the universe not to spill the news to her before I had a chance. She'd never understand, and worse, she'd likely never believe me. I hadn't even had any time at all to knock down those walls before another lie came in, threatening to end whatever we'd started.

11

KELLY

My neck hurt, and my jaw too. I was so exhausted from talking with Mr. and Mrs. Davenport that I just wanted to curl up into a tiny ball and take a nap. We had been out to coffee for two hours before my growling stomach drove them to suggesting lunch, and I'd wanted to scream at that point.

I had stood up, sweetly declining, telling them I had brought lunch and just needed to head back to the shelter, but they insisted. I wasn't versed enough in turning down deep pockets, especially when Aubrey was texting intermittently, checking to see how it was going. I knew it was super late in Australia, so it was obviously a big deal to her.

Once I was finally free, I texted Julie that I was heading home for the day. I was sitting on the bench, waiting for the bus when someone's deep exhalation startled me. I looked up, clutching my cell to my chest in fear.

A pair of sparkling blue eyes met me.

"Shit, you scared me." I heaved, sagging in my seat. Greyson had his hands shoved into his pockets, his corded forearms on display thanks to his rolled sleeves. The night before came rushing back, making heat simmer under my skin, burning me inside and out.

"When are you going to accept that I am not letting you ride the bus anymore?" he asked, tilting his head toward the sky. It was chilly, but a warm breeze was still lingering on the fringe.

"I didn't know that was a permanent thing. We had one encounter with me riding the bus home," I retorted, already annoyed with him.

"It's permanent. In fact"—he leaned closer—"even when you get your car back, I might still demand that you ride with me."

His seductive smile made me want to hide my flaming face in his neck. Instead, I stood, too tired to even argue with him.

"Okay, I'll take a ride." I pushed past him, heading toward his SUV.

He turned on his heel, falling in line behind me. "Just like that? No argument?"

He caught up to me on the sidewalk, his delicious scent wrapping around me like an overdue hug.

I stopped, huffing out an exhausted breath. "Just like that. I'm exhausted, so I'll go with you. I just want to take a nap."

He hung back for a second then rushed past me, unlocking the car and opening the passenger door for me. I slid in, already missing his proximity. I hated that I had fallen for him again so quickly. I was truly just flat-out disappointed in myself.

Greyson had shattered my heart a mere four years before and there I was, one hot-and-heavy kiss later, already missing him. I was foolish.

So fucking foolish.

"Do you need to stop anywhere before we head home?" Greyson asked, pulling away from the curb, not looking at me. He was slick, I'd give him that; he was lucky I let the 'home' comment fly.

"No, I just need a bed and some sleep." I yawned, wishing I'd gotten at least a little bit of sleep the night prior. "This is all your fault, by the way," I said, leaning my head against the window.

"My fault, how?" I could hear the smile in his voice.

"That kiss last night…the comment about the beach…I didn't get any sleep," I said sluggishly. The warm interior of the car and the smooth ride were rocking me to sleep, like a baby.

"Did you figure it out?" Greyson asked after a few silent beats. Maybe it was minutes…who knows.

I let out another yawn. "No…the only thing I remember from that trip is you kissing me a lot and telling me that if you could have this forever, you would."

I tried to think back to that weekend. It was one of the best of my life, and I remembered smiling the entire time. I remembered the butterflies that took flight when he made the forever comment. *Does that mean….?*

I tried to work it all out, like a math problem, but I was just too tired. I closed my eyes and let the darkness claim me.

Four years earlier
Greyson

The sound of the waves crashing against the shore echoed through every open window of the house. It was a three-story waterfront home that was owned by my family and tainted by my father's money. Being there with Kat felt so strange. She was more open to blending our worlds together than I was at first. We did bond over the fact that our families had hated each other for the last twenty years, but having her actually stay in something my father owned felt wrong.

I met Kelly Thomas back in private school when we were just kids. She was never on my radar, mostly because she clung to her sister Selah like she'd keel over and die if the two were ever separated. She wasn't much to look at then, anyway, and I had a short attention span.

Then, over time, I started to see her at some parties when we started high school, but she was still the tallish, gangly girl with straw-like hair who was way too quiet. It wasn't until our junior year that things changed for me. I noticed her long dark hair, her creamy complexion, her amazing rack that had grown plump and perfect. We had classes together and saw each other at parties on the weekends, but she never gave me the time of day.

Again, I didn't have much of an attention span, and by then, Dad had mentioned the Thomas's enough that I knew there was bad blood there, enough to make me steer clear of both her and her sister.

That was fine by me—until freshman year of college.

Of course she'd shown up at Berkeley. Of course she was pre-law. Of course she was a hundred times more gorgeous than she ever was in high school, and of course she just happened to be thrust into my world.

She went on one date with my roommate Neil. Just one.

I lived in the dorms at Berkeley to enjoy the full college experience and, more than anything, to get the fuck away from my father. Our dorm shared a common room, and we had separate bedrooms.

The night Kelly Thomas showed up with Neil, wearing a tight black dress that barely covered her ass, I knew she wouldn't be going out with him again. I told my roommate as much too.

I'd known her too long, had secretly wanted her longer, and essentially called dibs; all I needed to do was convince her of it.

"Hey, what are you thinking about?" Kat kissed my ear, wrapping her slender arms around my chest, bringing me out of my memories of how I'd started dating her.

"Just us." I brushed my fingers down her arms, loving the way her naked chest brushed against my bare back.

"What about us?" She pressed a kiss to my neck, running her fingers up through my hair, tugging on the ends. *Fuck.* I loved it when she touched me that way.

"How we met, how I took you from Neil...how you're mine now." I pulled her calf over my thigh, running my hand down her leg while she continued kissing my neck.

"I love that story," she whispered, moving down to my shoulders, branding me with her lips. My heart raced, like it did whenever I began to think about how our story had started and how I already knew, deep in my gut, how it would end.

Marriage.

Kat was still a little tipsy from her afternoon chardonnay. We'd fucked and napped nearly every day we'd been there, and though it was only three in the afternoon, I knew she was slightly drunk.

"I love that story too," I replied, reaching higher up on her thigh, pulling her closer.

She made a sound in the back of her throat, something close to a moan, which made my cock twitch.

"In fact, it's my favorite story." I brought her wrist to my mouth, kissing the inside of it softly. "Our forever story."

"Forever," Kat murmured into my shoulder, letting her tongue dart out, tracing a path of heat down my skin.

"I want forever with you, Kat. Weekends like this won't ever be enough for me—I'll always want more with you," I said in a rushed whisper, lacing my fingers with hers.

She made another sound, but before she could say anything in response, I tugged her until she was lying flat on the bed and I was hovering over her. I kissed her hard, moving my hand to her core, sinking a finger into her heat.

"Grey," Kat moaned, throwing her head back, bringing her hand to my neck then moving down, gripping my shoulder.

I leaned down, flicking her pebbled nipple with my tongue and sucking it into my mouth. Kat writhed against my hand, silently begging me for another finger. I sank in two more, rubbing her clit with my thumb.

"God, yes, Grey." She tossed her head to the side.

This was part of why I knew I could never have anyone else. I'd never be the same after Kat. What I'd been feeling for the past month was cemented; I was past falling in love—I was fucking gone for this woman. I needed her to be with me for the rest of my life. I knew we were young, knew we'd just started college. I knew all this and still I couldn't push past the idea of making her my wife.

I wanted her forever, regardless of when that started or when we did it. I just needed her to say yes.

12

KELLY

I BLINKED MY EYES OPEN, trying to get my bearings. Darkness met me as my eyelashes fluttered...which was strange. I sat up, rubbing my face, trying to assess the room.

All I could really see were blankets, a dark dresser and television on the far wall, and a large window covered with a thick blackout shade to my right. A side table was on my left and my cell rested there, on the edge, but for whatever reason, I wasn't eager to reach for it.

I moved my fingers along the soft blankets toward the center of the bed until I was creeping along the edge, where Greyson slept. I assumed it was Greyson, at least; his scent was on the sheets, tempting me to inhale them awkwardly loudly. God, I missed his smell. It was the perfect blend of spice and citrus and all those delicious things that were distinctly male.

I pressed against the hard, bare chest of the man who had apparently kidnapped me, trying to wake him gently.

"Why are you awake?" Greyson tiredly asked, shifting his body until he was on his side, facing me.

"Where am I?" I whispered, trying to get closer.

"Why are you whispering?"

"Because I don't know where I am...I have no idea what kind of conditions we're in."

"What is that supposed to mean?" He laughed, sleepily and so adorably my heart nearly exploded. This right here, these kinds of moments, drenched in darkness, absolved of all light from the previous day with no indication that tomorrow would even come...I missed having those with him.

I swallowed the feelings that were causing my chest to constrict. "What if there's a jealous fiancée behind the door who decides to come running after me with an axe because she heard me whispering in the dark with her man?"

His throaty laugh moved closer to me, making me uneasy. Sadly, I wasn't joking about my fear. I had no idea what Greyson's love life currently looked like. He'd mentioned that he wanted a chance, that he wanted me back...but did that mean he was officially single? Or was he dating some fabulous model with legs ten feet long and spiky heels?

I'd kissed him the night before, but stupidly and regrettably, I hadn't asked him about his dating life.

Warm breath coasted across my neck as his words hit my ear. "There's no fiancée."

A rush of heat to my core. The finality in his tone sent angry shivers down my arms.

His lips brushed the shell of my ear. "No girlfriend."

A firm hand grabbed my hip, pulling me closer to him. My breath stalled in my lungs as his warm chest brushed against my shirt. It was as though I wasn't even wearing one.

"You're in my bed, I'm the only person who has ever slept in it…and you're the only person I ever want in it." His lips brushed against mine quickly, in a rushed panic, like he was requesting access, like he'd die without it.

The door I had slammed on us all those years ago rattled and shook, begging to be opened again. I could feel the full weight of the decision in my chest, like a little baby elephant sitting there squashing me, daring me not to die.

This wasn't a good idea. Greyson wasn't a good idea. If I were to bet on the outcome of this situation, I'd say the odds were going to fuck me over. I knew better than this.

But…

I may not have trusted him with my heart, but damn he'd always been so good to my body.

Decision made, I leaned forward, covering his mouth with my own.

Firm hot hands traced a line down my back, over my shirt as they pulled me even closer. His hips shifted the slightest bit, revealing his hardness, which felt ridiculously unfair since he was apparently only in a pair of boxer briefs.

I slanted my mouth, already desperate for more of him. He broke our kiss seconds later, his lips disappearing and trailing down my neck. It happened so fast it nearly shocked me.

He pushed me into the mattress as he continued marking my skin, popping buttons on my shirt with ease. As soon as it was undone entirely, he sat up, staring down at me. My chest was rising and falling in unhealthy succession.

I was wearing a simple black bra, nothing crazy sexy about it, but the way he carefully traced a line down the center of my chest and over my pebbled flesh made me feel irresistible, sexy in a way I hadn't in years.

The pad of his finger brushed along the fabric covering my nipple, forcing it to harden to a painful degree. I ached for him to pull the cup of my bra down and touch the skin there.

He kept tracing lines into my skin, all along the inside dip of my cleavage, up to my throat, across my lips. He brushed back stray strands of my hair as he moved that finger back down, over my breasts, down my navel, to my belly button, along my ribs.

It was torture. I wanted him to remove my clothing, to touch me in a way only he could. Sure, I'd mentally and physically tried to move on after our breakup, but no man had made me feel the way Greyson did. It might have had to do with the fact that my heart still belonged to the idiot, but either way, I hadn't felt this way since him.

"Don't move. I just want to touch you, Kat." He spoke so close to my ear as he leaned on his arm, tracing lines into my skin.

I nodded my acceptance, not that he was really asking for it.

Desperation clung to me like a second skin as I clenched my thighs together.

Three fingers drifted along my chest before they dipped under the material covering my breasts.

I inhaled a sharp breath as he cupped me, refusing to draw the material down. His thumb roughly rubbed against my hardened nipple, and his fingers came together to squeeze it, making me gasp.

"Still like that, huh?" he asked, voice sultry and dark, like the darkness in the room had wrapped around his vocal cords, like he was going to ruin me tonight and I could do nothing about it.

"Yes," I moaned as he pinched it again. I wanted his mouth on me, wanted him to take me in, lap his wet tongue over my sensitive nub.

But I wouldn't beg. I refused to beg.

His hand left that breast, moving to the other one, and he repeated the process, still not pulling the material down, which only made me want it more.

His hand flattened against my back as he drew closer to the waistline of my skirt. Slowly he began dragging the zipper down, one inch at a time. The entire process was so slow and so methodical it nearly made me come.

All I could hear was our labored breathing, as if these slow touches were drawing out more sexual exertion than him being inside of me would.

Once my skirt was pulled down, his hand returned to my stomach. Slowly moving his hand lower, he dipped under my simple, black, bikini-style cotton underwear.

He ran those fingers down, over my pubic bone, until he was tracing my slit.

I hissed on instinct because, *fucking hell*, it felt so good to be touched.

He didn't push his fingers inside, just carefully ran them up and down my aching folds.

"Greyson." I moaned in a breathy panic. He needed to touch me.

I hadn't realized how much I'd longed for his touch, how much I missed it.

"Do you like that?" he asked, light and soft. He knew what he was doing. Fuck him, he knew.

"Yes," I pathetically moaned. "But I need more," I declared, ensuring that I wasn't begging. No, this was more businesslike, as though he was merely serving up some ice cream and I just needed one more scoop.

His slid one finger dangerously close to my clit, feeling how wet and ready I was. He moaned, lowering his head to my chest.

"You're fucking soaked."

Did he think there'd be any other response to him? The moment Greyson first placed his lips against my body, it was like he'd stolen it from ever belonging to anyone else. Whether he wanted it or not, it belonged to him.

He pushed a finger inside me, slowly drawing it in and out, knowing he was torturing me.

I broke down and begged. "Greyson, please."

"I love the way my name sounds on your lips," he rasped into the darkness.

I moved my head to the side, feeling like I was coming out of my skin, gripping the sheets in anticipation. My eyes slid closed, as though keeping them shut would protect me from revisiting old memories.

He continued pushing his fingers in and out of my center slowly, drawing out my moans and whispered curses.

"Yes, baby, that's it. Let me hear you," he murmured before inserting another finger, rubbing at my clit, forcing my hips to rock in rhythm with his ministrations against my wet center.

A myriad of curse words swam through my head as white spots blinked behind my closed eyelids.

"Come for me, baby," he whispered, leaning down to kiss me. His tongue swept into my mouth, hot with desire and desperation. He worked his hand inside me, drawing out my pleasure while he kissed me recklessly.

I couldn't handle it anymore. I used my right hand and covered his hand, which was down my underwear, pushing on it to add pressure. I rode his hand, letting him fuck me with his fingers while I came harder than I had in four long years.

A delirious feeling washed over me, stronger than my orgasm, stronger than the cherished feeling I'd always had with Greyson. I realized in the darkness of his room that I still loved him. More importantly, I was still *in* love with him, and that left me entirely fucked.

13

GREYSON

I was sure I had whiplash. Maybe I'd been in an accident and I was dreaming or in a coma, because I had been nearly positive that this night was headed in a different direction.

Instead of sinking my dick inside the woman I was in love with and starting to bridge the gap between us, I was staring at the closed bathroom door.

For the millionth time, I replayed it in my head. I was there, in the dark, making her come while she moved against my fingers. She was begging me, cursing me, groaning for me, everything going fucking perfectly. I had plans for us after the finger session. We would move to all kinds of different positions—but then, as if the lights had flicked on, she pushed against my hand and flipped over, scurrying to the bathroom, and she hadn't come out since.

I had no idea what the hell had happened, or where I'd gone wrong. Maybe I'd gone too fast, but she had seemed into it. I'd even gone slowly. I had been careful, too, making sure she was with me every second of the way.

The lock clicked from inside the bathroom, and my head swung up in time to see the door open. Kat was there, her cherry red lips had just a clear sheen over them, her makeup had been fixed, her shirt was tucked into her jeans, and her high heels were back on her feet. She started for the front door like she was on a mission, forcing me to stand and latch onto her elbow.

"Where are you going?"

She wouldn't meet my eyes. Her dark hair was over her shoulder, but the tangles from being in bed with me were still there. It almost made me smile. Instead, I focused on her chin, wanting so badly to tip it up so those eyes would show me what was really going on.

"Home," she replied easily.

"Did I miss something?" I scoffed, feeling horribly vulnerable. It was like I had handed her my heart, and she'd tossed it from hand to hand, considering what to do before just throwing it to the ground and stomping on it.

"It's just…" Clearing her throat, she finally met my eyes. "I wasn't ready for this, for coming here…for that." She glanced back toward my bedroom.

"Okay, that's no big deal. You could have just put the brakes on in there and I would have stopped." I shuffled closer, needing to be near her.

"I know you would have…it's just…" She faltered for a second, bringing her fingers to her hair, toying with the ends.

"It's just what?"

Tell me. Tell me what's going on in your mind, in your head. Let me see you.

She moved her mouth as if she was about to say something then shook her head back and forth, like she was dismissing the thought as quickly as it had come.

"Kat, come on," I said to her back as she pushed past me again. *Fuck.* "Is it the boyfriend?" I asked, already knowing that whole thing was bullshit.

Her eyes grew wide before she bit on her lip. "No...god. I'm not..." She shifted from foot to foot. "I'm not actually seeing anyone...I was lying about that."

Fucking knew it. "Then what?"

"It's not personal. I just have to go," she muttered, pulling open my front door and storming through it.

An Uber was already pulled up to my curb, ready and waiting. Kat opened the back door and crawled in, and within seconds, it was driving away.

I stood there, watching the taillights disappear down the street, feeling like an idiot.

I hated how close I kept getting to having her only to have it ripped away faster than I could grasp it. I wanted to call Josh and talk about where he thought I might have gone wrong. For all his faults, he had an oddly good sense of understanding where women he wasn't screwing were concerned. Still, I didn't feel like running back through the night only to find out it was blaringly obvious that Kat wasn't into me.

I couldn't handle it, couldn't even consider that she didn't actually want me—not when it felt so real when she was under me, at the mercy of my touch, not when it was so obvious that she still felt something for me.

I ran a hand through my hair and called in the only distraction I could think of.

I dialed the number I'd kept avoiding in my phone and put it up to my ear.

"Hey, I know it's late, but could I see him tonight? Yeah, go ahead and bring his stuff. I'm ready to have him permanently."

14

KELLY

I FELT like I had a hangover. It was ridiculous and unfair because I hadn't had a sip of alcohol to help temper my stupid heart and all its thrashing it did after I tucked tail and ran from Greyson's.

I wore a minimal amount of makeup, put my hair in a top knot, and donned jeggings. Don't even ask why, but in addition to feeling like I had a hangover, I also felt bloated and uncomfortable in everything.

It was like my skin was too tight but also too big for my bones at the same time. I didn't want to confront the revelation I'd had the previous night while gyrating against the hand of my ex-boyfriend.

The same feeling I'd had then was still sitting like a block of cheese in my chest.

"Good morning, Kelly!" Payton said, way too loudly. Since when was she calling me by my first name?

"Morning," I said with a tight smile and my sunglasses still plastered to my face. Everything was too bright.

"You have a surgery scheduled with Dr. Knox around ten. He said it's a bigger breed animal and to be sure to wear closed-toe shoes."

Since when was Payton playing assistant? It was always Julie who told me about my schedule.

I wanted to stomp my foot in frustration over how unfair it was that I was currently working with my ex and therefore couldn't just lick my wounds in private. Also, there was the startling, stupid fact that I was still in love with the idiot. I didn't want to be doing surgeries or having to stand next to him while saving animals.

"Also, sorry, Julie said to tell you all this stuff because she's running behind in getting here. She said it was something to do with yoga, but, shoot…she said not to tell you that part." Payton shuffled her notes around, running after me. I wasn't even in the mood to slow down to hear the rest, so she was clicking along the laminate in her ridiculously tall heels. "Um, but Julie said to tell you that you have a video call with Aubrey later too and…uh…sorry, these heels are hard to run in."

I swung my office door open, hoping she'd somehow be thwarted by it closing behind me.

She wasn't.

Situating myself in the chair at my desk and pulling my sunglasses off with force, I put my face in my hands while Payton kept talking.

"So, Aubrey wants both you and Greyson in on the call today."

I looked up, suddenly appalled by her mere existence.

"What?"

Payton's light eyebrows drew together in confusion. "Uh, yeah...um..." She shuffled a few notes then re-read one of them. "Yeah, it says Greyson will be on the call with you."

I wanted to call Aubrey and tell her no—no to Greyson, and maybe could we just fire him?—but I remembered we hadn't even technically hired him, so what the fuck was I supposed to do with that?

"Okay, thank you," I muttered, feeling my shoulders sag in defeat.

Payton stayed rooted to the faded blue carpet in my office. The rest of the shelter was adorned in a gorgeous oak-colored laminate wood flooring—why the hell had they skipped my office when sprucing the place up?

"Can I help you with anything else?" I blinked slowly, trying to hide my souring expression.

"It's just..." Payton shuffled from one foot to the other like she had to pee. I was two seconds away from asking if she needed to tinkle.

"Yes?" I encouraged her. *Out with it. Talk, so I can slam my face against the desk!*

"You guys are such a cute couple...and I just wanted you to know I'm totally team Grelley...or Kayson?" She tilted her head to the side, raising a blonde brow.

In response, I could feel my brows scrunch together in confusion. What the hell was she talking about?

"Wha..." The words died on my tongue as Greyson rapped his knuckles on the doorframe of my office. Payton beamed at him, flushed red, and scampered off as the front desk phone started ringing.

My chest constricted tightly as those blue eyes lit with fire, desperate to burn me from the inside out. He wanted answers, an explanation as to what the hell had happened the night before, and I just wanted to forget the entire thing because that would be so much easier than facing the truth.

"Glad you made it in okay," he started. His voice was gruff, like he hadn't slept well, which was my fault. I had run out of his house at nearly one thirty in the morning.

I toyed with the pen in front of me as I nodded. I couldn't even speak. *Fuck.*

He assessed me for a second longer, waiting for something. We both knew if he wanted to force the conversation, all he would have to do is shut that door, lock it, and walk over here. I wasn't even close to strong enough to resist him if he touched me.

"Just making sure you got the memo about the surgery today. It's on a Great Dane that came in last night. We think he was hit by a car."

My heart wilted. Poor thing.

I stood, noticing the strain in Greyson's voice, the tightness in his eyes.

"You okay with doing this surgery?" I asked, remembering when his Great Dane had died and how much it had impacted him. He didn't have the easiest life with his family, but that dog…he'd had it forever, and from what I remembered, Dutch had been special to him.

Greyson's expression softened, his blue eyes alight with curiosity as he searched my face.

I could feel the fire build between us, his unspoken words flickering in the empty space between us like he was striking a match, hoping to find a flame.

Unfortunately, I refused to let it catch fire.

He must have sensed my emotional shutdown because he cleared his throat and shook his head.

"It'll be fine. Just need an assistant, and if you won't be able to do it, I'll have to find someone else."

That comment landed like a long-distance jumper in quicksand. It was stuck, sinking farther the more I tried to move it around in my head.

I knew he was talking about the surgery, but I felt the deeper meaning. *I'll have to find someone else.*

"I'll be there," I said dryly, desperate to end this strange interaction. I hated the awkwardness.

I should have shut him down the previous night. I should have woken and left the second I realized I was in his bed. I blinked, hoping to keep the stinging sensation behind my eyes at bay a little longer.

Greyson left, shutting the door while hopefully shutting down whatever this was between us. I didn't want a repeat of history; I wouldn't survive it.

The surgery went smoothly, and Greyson ended up asking one of the volunteers to step in to help us. They acted as a barrier between us and took on the brunt of the random conversation. Jason, the seventeen-year-old senior, was actually grateful for the opportunity since he was headed to college in the fall and planning to pursue a degree in veterinary medicine.

My stupid heart softened at what was clearly Greyson creating an opportunity for Jason.

The camera crew was there, filming like usual for our ever-growing YouTube channel, and I noticed them trying to zoom in on me and subsequently Greyson. I wasn't an idiot; I knew our channel was more popular because the fans thought something was happening between Greyson and me, but it wasn't.

It would be better to put an end to all of that sooner rather than later anyway. I felt better knowing we could potentially work together like this, someone in as a buffer between us, taking the focus off of us.

"You ready for this video call?" Greyson asked conversationally while we finished washing up at the large basin sink in the back.

His scrubs were still nearly immaculate and clung to him in such a way that showed off his defined muscles. I itched to run my finger down his throat, over that Adam's apple that seemed to move when he was staring at me. Scratch that—I wanted it to be my tongue that ran down the column of his throat, dipping into the V cut of his smock.

"Yeah," I replied awkwardly, and he probably sensed the roughness of my voice, breathy with desire. It seemed my earlier morning determination to stay free and clear of Greyson was starting to wear off. I needed a reinforcement.

As we tossed our paper towels in the trash, I sought out Julie, hoping my assistant was actually available to assist me for once.

Greyson veered toward my office, but I detoured toward the break room.

I found Julie looking over a procedure book while stirring her coffee.

"Hey, I need you," I said, hating the rushed desperation that was in my tone.

She blinked, her dark hair in a half ponytail, frizz exploding everywhere. "For what?"

I pulled her arm. "No time, I'll explain later. I just...ugh, I need you to take notes in this video call with Aubrey."

I dragged her toward the hallway, her heels nearly digging into the floor.

"Geez, okay. I'm coming." She finally relented and huffed her way to my office.

Julie pulled up an extra chair, avoiding Greyson, who was already seated in the chair across from my desk. As my assistant got herself a notepad and pen, I turned the computer monitor so we could all see the screen for when Aubrey called.

Greyson sat forward with his elbows on his knees as I clicked to connect to the online meeting, and there was a beat of awkward silence in the room as Greyson swung his gaze to Julie and back to me. His nose flared while those blue eyes dug into me. He knew why I had pulled Julie in here; he knew I was avoiding being alone with him.

Suddenly Aubrey's voice cut through the awkward silence, making me jump.

"Hey, sorry!" she apologized as I recovered, and I shook my head, feeling stupid for jumping.

"No worries, Aub. Sorry about that, just been a crazy day." I shuffled a pile of papers to emphasis my fake point.

"Sorry, won't keep you guys long. Hey Greyson, how are you?" Aubrey smiled at him, her dark auburn hair shifting across her tan shoulder. I had nearly forgotten it was summertime over there.

Greyson smiled. "Hey there, nice to see you," he said cordially.

I didn't know where Chance was, but knowing they were in Australia visiting his family, I figured he was likely with them.

"Well, I want to get right to the point, as I don't want to take any more time away from you guys. Julie, thank you for being here as well. Kel, that was a great idea, as there will be a ton of notes to take."

Julie, in response, smiled and got her pen in position over the tablet in front of her.

Aubrey leaned back, smiled again, and pulled out a piece of paper then began reading.

"I am so excited to share with you guys that our shelter—and, more specifically, the two of you, Greyson and Kelly—have been invited to the first ever 'Save a Shelter' benefit ball. It's a black tie event, super glitzy, it will include all of Temecula's and some of LA's elite, and it's all to support the Park Street Animal Shelter."

I hadn't exactly checked out, but my overeager brain was starting to turn all the information over and over. A black tie event with Greyson. Greyson in a fitted suit. Greyson with a date. My stomach clenched tight.

"Kelly, did you hear me, girl? Did the video cut out?" Aubrey asked, touching her screen like the little girl in braces tapping the glass fish tank in *Finding Nemo*.

I cleared my throat. "Sorry, just processing. This is huge news. Massive. This will be a game changer for sure." I spoke with as much pep as I could muster. I really was excited for our shelter. There were several things I had hopes for budget-wise, a dream board of things I wanted to do and new things I wanted to add. If we could afford to purchase the warehouse attached to the back of our building, it would allow us to take in even more animals and provide for them on a longer-term basis since we were proudly a no-kill shelter.

"So, the details. Like I said, it's black tie, and this part might get a little weird, but honestly none of this would be possible without Greyson or his connections." She paused with her hand out toward his side of the desk, and he smiled in response. "So, with that said…it's no secret that you guys have stirred up the media train and caught the attention of nation-wide news. Because of that, I'm asking that you don't bring dates to this event. I'm asking that you go with each other and present a united front. In a way, I'd like you to keep up the image that you guys are…" She trailed off, a small blush over-whelming her face.

Was she asking that we sell ourselves as a couple so more people would donate money?

"God no!" Aubrey said quickly.

Shit, did I ask that out loud?

"Just…it's just that it would seem a bit more unified if you went together. You absolutely do not have to act like or say that you are a couple. I just thought it would look a little stronger, more of a team effort if you were there together without dates."

Aubrey's hands came together, and she looked like the poised lawyer I knew her to be. It was a pose she assumed when she was trying to find a creative solution between two parties. It made me miss her so much. We used to eat lunch together, whenever she wasn't with Richard, the boyfriend she had while I knew her, the one before she dated Chance—or, as I learned later, the one she dated *after* Chance, before the Australian model came back for his girl and fought for her.

Not having to see Greyson with a date would make the night more bearable, so I smiled to encourage Aubrey. I didn't want her to think I was against the idea. Before I could say anything, a white head of fur came into the screen, munching something green.

"Oh my god! Pixy, no!" Aubrey shrieked. "That was Grammy's favorite plant. Your daddy is going to be so pissed when he finds out you ate it. Have some respect for your grandmother's house!" she said while turned away from the camera. She scooted toward the edge, patting the head of the animal while it bleated at her. "Mommy's on a call, so I need you to behave. Your father will be back soon. Go back to your spot by the door." She leaned in and kissed the white fur of the animal before returning to us. "Sorry about that." She blushed.

Greyson sat up straight, his hand toward the screen, confusion apparent on his face. "Was that a goat?"

"Uh, yeah…our kid. No pun intended. Um, we actually have a human kid on the way, but Pixy was our first kid and still travels everywhere with us." Aubrey laughed nervously. "Anyway, so, let's get back to this. I'm going to email Julie the address, date, and time. There will be a moment for you both to give a little speech about the animal shelter, and please just know how excited I am about this. Ever since I left Hermosa Beach, I've ached to fulfill the animal-shelter-shaped hole inside me. So, I've been vicariously living through all the action happening over there. Do you guys have any questions?" Aubrey asked, still patting Pixy, who hadn't gone off to his corner as instructed.

Greyson stood, hunching over the desk. "I think we're good. I'll watch for the email from Julie with dates and the time. It sounds like it'll be fun." He winked at me then walked out the door.

"Okay, great. I can't wait to see the footage of all of it. We already cleared it with the host and sponsors who are putting on the benefit, so it'll be no problem to have our camera guys there."

Since when were they *our* camera guys? They were Greyson's camera guys, and he happened to be offering himself for free for the benefit of the shelter.

My mind churned again with too many unanswered questions. I needed to talk to him, needed to sit down and have a real conversation with him.

I let out a heavy sigh after ending the call with Aubrey and thanking Julie. I sat back in my chair, pulling my cell free, ready to face something I'd avoided since Greyson came back.

15

GREYSON

Kelly had avoided me all day, though not physically. She was there...but not. Her eyes were vacant, her smile empty, and her words were missing any real depth. She was going to pretend like the previous night hadn't happened.

I wondered if she'd talk to me, really talk, but it was clear she wasn't interested.

After that video call with Aubrey, my mind was moving too fast to stay in the shelter. I wasn't needed there for the rest of the day, so I told Payton I would be on call if any emergency cases came in. Then I started toward downtown on foot.

The idea of having Kelly to myself all evening, dressed to the nines, was enticing to say the least. I craved time with her, any chance to go somewhere new, getting us back to the relationship like we had in the past, but the night before was still blasting on repeat in my head. She was there, under me, moaning and expectant, desire clearly curling around us.

Then something had happened, and I wanted to know what it was and how to fix it.

I was nearly past the parking lot of the shelter when my phone pinged.

Kelly: Can we go somewhere to eat? And talk, maybe?

I stared at the screen, feeling a smile creep along my face.

Me: Yes, I'm leaving now. Can you get away for a bit?

Kelly: Yes, I'll come to the parking lot. Maybe we can go to that diner down a few blocks?

Me: Sounds good.

I pocketed my phone and headed toward my car, waiting for her.

A few minutes later, she pushed through the glass doors. She had the same smile on her face that she'd had the night before in the hallway, the same look in her eye that she'd had earlier in the day after the surgery. She was resisting me, but she wasn't entirely immune to me, which made my chest burn with excited energy. There was hope for us.

Kat stirred her coffee, her dark hair falling around her face like a silken sheet. She pushed the strands back, behind her ear, smiling down at her drink. I wanted to lean forward and feel it between my fingers.

"So, you wanted to talk?" I asked, sipping my own coffee. We'd gone to the diner like she suggested, but it seemed neither of us had much of an appetite. Mine was currently only for her mouth, or more of her body.

Kat looked up, her eyes bright and expectant.

"I wanted to talk…literally just talk. I think part of what happened last night was that you acted like nothing had happened between us in four years, like we could just pick back up where we left off."

Is that what she thought? The way her eyes darted around the table told me there was more to it than that, but it at least gave us a good place to start. I sat back, about to talk about last night, where I was coming from, and how there was no way in hell I assumed we'd just pick back up—but she spoke up, changing the subject.

"I mean, a ton of stuff has happened, Grey. Like, for instance, I have no idea why you chose to become a veterinarian. Last time I saw you, you were dead set on becoming a lawyer." She leaned forward, her spoon out to the side. Her eyes were bright and curious.

I loved that she wanted to know more about why I was there. It meant she cared.

About to respond, I sat forward, but she started back up with even more questions.

"And why this shelter? Why come back here at all if you weren't going to work with your father's firm?" She sipped her coffee, blinking rapidly. I could imagine her thoughts tangling together like a thick vine of ivy in her head.

"You finished?" I asked, laughing a bit. My chest felt light because these questions meant she wanted to retrace the broken steps of our past. She wanted to know about me. She was curious, and that was definitely moving in the right direction.

"Sorry, I'm a little spastic." She laughed nervously.

"First of all, that's a lot of conversation to fit into one afternoon. Why don't we start at the beginning then meet a few more times to finish up the rest?" Hoping she didn't try to read too much into it, I kept a stoic smile on my face. Besides, if she did try to read more into me asking for more dates, all she'd find is me desperate for more time with her. She wanted my story, and I wanted her. Plain. Simple. Just her.

"I suppose that wouldn't be the worst thing." She smiled into her coffee.

I kicked my leg out under the table and felt her leg press into mine, her eyebrows jumping at the contact.

That's right, I'm coming for you, baby.

"When you last saw me, I had planned on going to law school. I had plans to work with my father, but everything changed shortly after you left. I had some time to reflect, and I realized the lawyer thing was my father's dream, not mine. So, I left and pursued veterinary medicine instead."

I shrugged as if it was no big deal when in fact, it was the biggest deal of my life, save for when she left.

It was on the tip of my tongue to explain to her what had happened with my dad, what I had learned, but the truth was too complicated. When I humiliated her in front of everyone we knew, all her potential employers, I told her to never set foot on our side of town again. I told her not to show up in our social circles, or at our parties. I promised she'd be a pariah, and she was.

No one would touch her.

I couldn't merely look her up and say I was sorry. A grand gesture had to be made, but I had no idea how to do that while she was so angry and hurt. I had heard she'd left the country for a few months, traveled, lived her life without me, did a few of the things we had planned to do together. For all her hate and hurt toward me, she never blocked my social media accounts, so I was able to stalk her as much as I wanted to. It was creepy as fuck since she never knew, but I was madly in love with her, so there was nothing to be done.

So, I went on living and learning, adjusting to my new life. I stayed single, because I had been pining away for the girl I'd forced out of my life. When I saw that she'd started at the animal shelter, I knew it was my chance—my grand gesture.

Problem was, it wasn't as grand as I had hoped it would be.

"So, you just changed your entire career path and that was that?" Kat asked, curious as always, but there was something more to her tone.

"Yeah...something like that." I leaned forward, bringing our faces closer. "It was after an enlightening conversation with my father."

I watched her eyes. I wanted her to say it, to confess that she cared what that conversation was and ask why I was really here. I didn't want her to care about the line of work I chose. I wanted her to care about the fact that I *chose* her and there was a specific reason why.

Kat dipped her eyes to the table.

"Well, whatever that conversation was, I'm glad you found what makes you happy."

I stared at her, watching for something, anything to show that she knew it was her that I wanted, but her eyes were vacant...reluctant.

"I'm getting there." I leaned back, letting out a heavy sigh. Fuck, this was exhausting. Because of how much I'd messed everything up between us in the past, I was nervous as hell to fess up to everything that had happened. Would she even believe me? Would that somehow make it worse?

Kat's phone dinged, sitting next to her cup. She glanced down briefly, swiping her finger across the screen.

"Shit. I totally forgot." She stood quickly, shuffling out of the booth, and as I watched, I felt this strange sensation in my chest, like she'd plucked the strings in my heart and pulled.

"Where are you going?"

She shoved her phone into her purse, leaving her head dipped and her hair like a wall around her. I wanted inside of it. I wanted nothing between us anymore.

"My sister's—I totally forgot I said I'd babysit for them." She muttered a few more things while closing up her purse.

Her blue eyes found mine, likely remembering she didn't have a ride. My smile was slow. "I'll take you."

I'd also be staying and playing house with her for the night, whether she wanted me to or not. I wasn't losing any more time or ground with Kat. We'd take this as slow as she wanted, but we were happening.

16

KELLY

"Um, thank you for the ride," I mumbled as Greyson exited the car with me. Was he going to walk me all the way to my sister's door?

"No problem, glad to help." He shoved his hands into his pockets, all while eyeing the brick townhome in front of us.

Was I supposed to tell him to leave? Holy awkward of awkward moments. I could feel panic begin to surge as we neared Selah's door. I could hear the sounds of my nephews yelling on the other side as I made my way up the steps.

I often wondered how my sister's neighbors dealt with all the noise. While they were high-end townhomes, they sat so close to each other they practically shared a wall. My sister had the good sense to put the boys' rooms on the opposite end of the house so as not to share the nearest wall with her elderly neighbor.

I pulled my key free from my purse and began unlocking the door, knowing it would just irritate my sister if I rang the doorbell. It would get all the kids running toward it, and the dog too. It would take five minutes for her to pick her way to the front.

"So, thanks again. I guess I'll see you tomorrow at work." I turned to face Greyson, shoving out of my shell of subtlety. He wasn't staying, so why was he still standing there?

Hands still deep in his pockets, shoulders taut, Greyson merely smiled, making his side dimple pop and forcing me to nearly swallow my tongue. He reached around me, crossing the front of my body with his own, and he turned the handle then pressed the door open.

We poured into the chaos, my sister stopping mid-step while yelling at her sons to get off the couches and putting an earring in her ear.

Her blue eyes bounced from me to Greyson just seconds before a flashy, secretive smile broke out across her face.

Great. She had ideas. I didn't like those ideas.

"Greyson, oh my gosh, it's been forever!" She stepped closer to him.

He smiled, grabbing her in a hug that practically engulfed her. "Hey Selah, nice to see you again."

I stood behind Greyson, so Selah had a good look at my face. I narrowed my eyes and ran my finger across my throat, indicating that later tonight, I would so be killing her. I couldn't believe she was playing fond and happy with Greyson. Our family hated the Knoxes. Hated them! She'd refused to even look at any of Greyson's older brothers or cousins because the blood was that bad between us.

"Are you here to help Kel babysit?" She flicked her gaze from him to me as they broke apart. I wanted to pull her aside and punch her in the face.

Greyson said, "Yes," right as I said, "No."

We looked at each other, him giving me a hard stare, that unmoving glare that spoke louder than his words would. He was staying, no questions about it.

I let out a sigh as I could feel my reservations fall away. I shrugged out of my coat, laying it on the entryway bench, and then moved toward the chaos. I knew my sister wanted to pull me aside and ask for details; I could see it written all over her face as her eyebrows pinched together and her eyes bounced between Greyson and me.

"Alright, we're going to be late if we don't leave right this second," Bryan said pointedly to my sister, likely reading her reaction to Greyson showing up with me. He knew her too well. She was two seconds from throwing her evening out and dragging me down the hall. She'd be texting me as soon as she got into the car.

"Right. Okay, love you kids, be good!" Selah yelled toward the three dark-haired menaces who were currently ripping every cushion off the couch.

They didn't even respond. Monsters.

Greyson didn't wait for me to make it awkward, just shoved out of his coat, took off his shoes, and began helping the boys build a tower out of couch cushions.

I watched Greyson wrap an ACE bandage around my nephew's stuffed gorilla. He'd been doing operations on each of their animals for the past hour. He had a plastic stethoscope around his neck and a bandana wrapped around his head; the boys said that's how doctors wear it on TV.

The night had gone off without a hitch. Greyson ordered dinner from DoorDash, which I said was considered a big party fail when it came to babysitting guidelines. Everyone knew you had to go through the grueling process of awkwardly making them food they wouldn't eat.

But Greyson merely smirked, leaned into my space, and whispered that the kids were going to love it. And they did.

The pizza was a huge hit with all the delicious add-ons and crazy sauce mixes—who knew, but boys love to dunk pizza in just about every kind of sauce. Greyson also built them a fort they could actually sit in while watching the Godzilla movie from the 90s—the really good one with Matthew Broderick.

The boys went crazy for it, ate every single bite of their food and then moved into surgery mode, where they stayed. Honestly, I felt a little like I was the outsider in the evening's situation, which was a crazy feeling. My nephews only asked me something when Greyson hesitated for the briefest of seconds—like when they asked if they could cut up all of their mother's scarves for bandages.

Otherwise, it was perfect. I wasn't exactly eager to play house with Greyson, so I stuck to my little side of the living room, which wasn't bombarded with boys and slings. I had wine, my Kindle, and a healthy respect for avoiding my ex-boyfriend's glances.

Did he want me to join in with them? Perhaps, but my poor heart could not and would not be able to resist the pretty picture it would undoubtedly paint. It would take tiny fibers of the night and recreate a masterpiece in my head, replaying the lovely image over and over until cold reality sank in.

Greyson Knox wasn't the settling down type, not the marriage type—not the anything type. He was off limits, which was why I was over here, far away from his charm, his laughter, and his scent.

Instead, I decided to think over the conversation we'd had in the diner, to consider the fact that he had just up and changed his career right after I left. What did that mean? What had happened, and what was with that conversation he had with his father?

The man, as far as I could remember, was an absolute asshole, but I had never really interacted with him to know if that was actually really true. I just remembered the look on his face that fateful day when Greyson broke up with me; I remembered the smallest smirk curving his lips.

I hadn't thought anything of it because my heart was shattered into a billion pieces, but...no, it was too long ago. I wouldn't read into it. It didn't make a difference.

The night ended sooner than I hoped. Once my sister stepped inside, I knew I was going to get bombarded about not answering any of her texts about Greyson. She didn't know that her husband had also texted me and asked me to kindly ignore his wife so he could properly date her without distraction. They didn't get enough time together, and honestly, I wasn't ready to talk to Selah about my feelings for my ex.

She knew all too well about all the pain he'd put me through. So, instead of telling Greyson to go home on his own and staying with my sister, I grabbed my coat and kissed her on the cheek, hugged my nephews, and headed outside.

"That was fun," Greyson said over his shoulder as he drove toward my side of town.

I smiled at the windshield. "Those boys are pretty fun."

"Yeah, they are." A brief pause. "You seemed quiet tonight." His eyes flitted from me to the windshield. What was he looking for? I still had no idea what he wanted from me. He said he wanted a chance, but to what extent?

"They were smitten with you—I was trying to stay out of the way."

Greyson pulled up to the curb outside my building, and my heart plummeted to my stomach as we exited the car. I'd already known Greyson would walk me to my door; what I didn't know was if he'd kiss me again. I squeezed my eyes closed as I punched in my building code and grabbed the glass door, swinging it open.

Greyson's warm presence hovered at my back as we walked toward the elevators. I didn't want him to kiss me. I didn't want to fall under his spell. I needed to stay strong, needed to remember that there was an ocean of heartache between us. He hadn't fixed any of it, had merely gotten in a boat and tried to cross it like nothing had ever happened.

Once we were at my door, I pulled my keys free.

"Thanks for the ride and for bringing me home." I smiled, determined to end the night there. I turned away from him right as his hand shot out, gently grabbing my shoulder.

"About our conversations…" he said softly, turning me toward him.

Right. *Shit.*

I pushed my hair behind my ear, took a few shallow breaths, and dared to match his stare.

He stepped closer, the heat from his body slamming into me. "Tomorrow, can I take you to breakfast?"

I blinked, picturing us waking up together, slow kisses, lazy but amazing sex, just like we used to do before going to breakfast… "Yeah, that sounds good."

Then, before I had a chance to even flinch, his lips were pressed to my hairline in a sweet kiss. He stayed there longer than a person would normally stay plastered to someone's skin, a million seconds passing between us, that ocean raging and roaring at what was still broken and turbulent, dividing us.

I stepped back, out of his embrace, away from him, to the safety of the metaphorical shore. I smiled, opened my door, and allowed it to shut between us.

17

KELLY

TRUE TO HIS WORD, Greyson arrived the next morning to take me to breakfast. I hadn't slept well, but I hadn't been sleeping well in general since Greyson stepped back into my life. My mind wandered to a thousand and one places as to why he was here, why he'd come back, why here of all places.

"Morning," Greyson said, pressing a quick kiss to the side of my mouth.

So, we were casually kissing now, were we?

"Morning," I murmured back. The kiss he'd left on my forehead the previous night was still stuck in my mind.

We drove to breakfast, a small intimate brunch place that was rumored to serve the best crepes in the entire world. Our conversation flowed easily enough, Greyson resting back against his chair, his blond hair tousled on top, like he'd woken up and just run his fingers through it. His strong jaw moved, popping as he chewed and sipped his coffee while we revisited the topic of why he'd become a vet.

I sat back, trying to calm down and not be affected by his closeness or his stories.

"It was Dutch. When he got sick, I remember wishing I knew how to help him, wishing I could fix him. Because even at night after we'd taken him to the vet's office, I would be up by his side, reading books on how to make him more comfortable."

I lifted a brow. "Books?"

He let out a throaty laugh, a small breeze winding through the patio, moving his white, cotton button-up just the slightest bit. My heart fluttered at how good he looked, the bright fabric against his tan skin and blue eyes...he was devastating. It was more than that, though—always had been. He was a genuinely good person, to his core. Kind, considerate...loyal.

Yet he threw me away so easily.

"Books. I always dragged books with me when I was with Dutch, figuring the laptop or even my cell would bother him. I didn't want to make things worse for him..." He smiled; his eyes bright. "I had a theory about cancer and cell phones, and since he was pretty far gone, I wanted him with me as long as possible."

My poor, devastated heart. It rapidly beat against my rib cage, begging me to lean forward and kiss this man. I pictured him there, loose sweats, white shirt, sorrow lining his face as he leaned against the kitchen cabinets, rubbing his Great Dane on the back, trying to comfort him.

"That's noble of you to have stayed by him like that," I said softly, too enthralled with the idea of falling in love with the same person twice and how stupid that likely made me.

"He was mine to protect, mine to keep...something I wish I had applied to the people in my life, not just my pets." His eyes softened, narrowing on me.

I had been his at one time too, yes, and his to protect, but he'd thrown me to the wolves.

I looked toward the grove of trees off to the side of the cottage-style restaurant. The sun was shining through the leaves, playing peekaboo with us.

"So, you left Berkeley *and* changed your major? How did your father feel about this development?" I changed the subject, trying to keep the topic of *us* at bay.

"I changed my major, transferring over to UC Davis to start on my vet schooling." Greyson cut into his crepe while I cut into my probably-more-delicious pancake. I liked listening to him talk about his life. Even though these were the parts of our lives that were supposed to be lived together, I still wanted to hear about it all.

I still wanted to see that look in his eye when he spoke about his career, becoming a vet, and getting his degree, graduating his first batch of schooling, how he felt about undergrad... there was so much I'd missed.

"My father..." Greyson tilted his head to the side, giving me that look, like he didn't want to tell me all the details. "He didn't exactly agree with my choice, but shortly after..." He paused.

Why is he pausing?

"After what?" I finally asked, after Greyson hesitated too long.

"Just after some stuff...stuff that was just too big to overcome, anyway." Greyson waved his hand around, as if to dismiss all the past that sat in between us. "He didn't have any say in what I did. Although, he did assume I'd come back after I graduated. He was so sure about it that he had my office readied, a nameplate and an assistant ready to go."

I smiled, leaning on my fist. "He must have been pretty shocked when you showed him your scrubs."

"He was. I'll never forget the look on his face when I told him if he wanted to talk to me, he had to come out to this farm that sat outside the city limits. He showed up in his five-piece suit, carrying a briefcase, and he almost fell over when he saw me with a massive glove on, my arm shoved inside a dairy cow's ass."

"Ewwwww, Grey, gross." I laughed, throwing a piece of bread at him. "Why were you out at a farm? I didn't peg you as a farmer vet."

Greyson laughed, his smile wide, his white teeth flashing. "In school we do all kinds of rotations, and we have to train on nearly every kind animal."

"Wait…you didn't go to law school then? Not at all?"

"No, just took those two law and economics classes freshman year." Greyson narrowed his eyes, sipping more of his coffee.

"So why on earth did your dad assume you could just pick up and be a lawyer with his firm?"

Greyson's eyebrows pinched together. "Uh…my father isn't exactly the most moral person. He was going to just put me there, like a puppet. Cases would have gone however he wanted, but I would have held shares in the company…an easy vote."

"That's terrible." I sat back, slightly shocked but not really surprised at all.

"Just another reason I needed to leave that life, that family…all of it." Our waitress came with the check, laying it on the table, refilling our waters and coffees.

Greyson pulled his wallet free, but I didn't want him to keep paying for every meal we shared, so I pulled mine out as well.

I grabbed the ticket and put my card down on top of it right as Greyson looked up.

"No way. I've got it." He reached for the ticket, but I moved it.

"Nope, you got the last one. This one is on me." I twisted to the side, bringing the ticket with me.

"Fine then, I'll just owe you dinner tonight," he said, leaning forward with a wicked gleam in his eye.

I wanted to say yes. I wanted to keep these meals and this conversation flowing, because I wanted to know all the tiny details of Greyson's life that I had missed. Unfortunately, I knew too well what would happen if I said yes to dinner. Greyson would find some way to take me home, he'd kiss me, and then I'd trip and open my goddam legs for him.

Because I was weak. So weak.

I swallowed the pain and the hope that tried to surface in my chest and slowly slid the ticket back toward Greyson's side of the table.

His face fell, his eyes narrowing into angry slits and his mouth becoming a thin line. I hated that expression on him, like I'd just said he couldn't have the one thing he wanted in life.

"Kat, please just—"

"How was everything?" Our waitress carefully grabbed his card and the white ticket, unknowingly cutting Greyson off.

"Great, thank you." I smiled back, encouraging her to move along and bring us back the receipt.

Once she hurried off, I met Greyson's stare head on, ready to defend my position.

"Dinners, breakfasts...I do want to talk, Greyson, but I don't want to fall into some habit where it feels like we're dating again. I don't want to get comfortable with you again."

That muscle in his defined jaw jumped as he ground his teeth together. He seemed a billion times broodier now, more guarded, as if a wall had just slipped between us.

Good.

Walls were good.

"Understood," he replied, cold and detached.

"All set. Thank you so much for coming in." The waitress came back with the leather billfold and a pen. She winked at Greyson before spinning around and leaving us alone.

He scribbled his signature and tip, flipped the leather shut, and stood.

I felt split, half of me wishing Greyson would call my bluff and tell me he wasn't backing off, tell me he'd still keep coming after me. The other half wished that when we left the restaurant, we'd go our separate ways for good.

"Kelly, we have a few more volunteers who just signed up to help out," Payton said, pulling my attention from my cell as I walked toward the dog kennels.

My heart hadn't been in a good place since Jet left, but I was trying to take that heartbreak and spend some time with our other rescues.

"That's like the fifth new one this week, right?" I asked, confused by all the new signups. Maybe this was normal, but from what I'd heard, getting volunteers to sign up was nearly as difficult as getting donations.

"Yep, number seven since Dr. Knox started." Payton smiled. I returned her smile with a tight one of my own, trying to focus on her golden hair tied back in big braids instead of the dreamy look she often got in her eyes when she talked about Greyson.

I halfheartedly responded, "Well, we started roughly around the same time, so maybe it's me."

I was kidding. Obviously, I knew it was Greyson that had drawn all the attention, but I wasn't ready to admit that.

"Yeah…that's what I meant. Since you both started here." Payton's eyes flitted around the room as a small blush crept up her neck.

"I'm joking, Payton. I know it's because of Greyson." I laughed, turning on my heel toward the kennels.

"I think it's really because of both of you. Just my opinion, but it's pretty swoony when he stares at you." That blush grew, invading her cheeks and close to her ears.

"He doesn't stare," I insisted, feeling my own blush creep up my neck.

"He does! Look, I know this is super creepy, but I accidentally caught it on camera once." She moved closer, pulling her phone free, then she pressed on the menu and brought up some file.

Was I really standing in the middle of an animal shelter while cats freely roamed, curling around my ankles, waiting for this girl I barely knew to pull up a video so I could see Greyson staring at me? *What on earth has my life come to?*

I watched as it started. It was of Payton doing a selfie video about what she was going to eat for lunch that day, and she was talking about macronutrients—super surprising based on the amount of sugar that went into her coffees. In the background you could see me talking with two new volunteers, going over some paperwork. Greyson stood behind me, where I couldn't see him, and his posture changed the second he seemed to realize I was busy and couldn't see him. He kept doing that cute duck and peek where he'd pretend to focus on what was in front of him but would lift his head to look at me every few seconds.

"Holy shit." I exhaled, grabbing Payton's phone.

"He does it all the time, and he did it a lot when you'd spend time with Jet," she added softly as I watched him flip that azure gaze up toward me, pausing with the smallest smile tugging on his lips. Dammit, there was that feeling in my chest, like one of the kittens had gotten inside my rib cage, tugged on my heart with its little paws, and started playing with my heartstrings, bundling them into a massive mess.

"This is sweet. Thanks for showing me, Payton," I said, my voice tight and controlled. Handing her the phone back, I straightened my shirt and ducked my head so no one could see my face. I needed to let this go, stop letting these feelings surface. I needed to lock this down, once and for all.

I continued my walk to the kennels, where I checked on the charts to see which dog needed a walk, grabbed a leash, and hooked up the Husky that had come in a few days prior. He was a good dog from what we could tell and knew basic commands, but he had a lot of energy.

I started heading out of the shelter, hopeful I didn't run into Greyson anywhere. Since our breakfast, things between us had been so awkward. He would talk to me, but it always felt strained, like there were words dancing on his tongue, desperate to spin their way into my ears, making room in my head and down to my heart.

We still had a week before the benefit dinner, where we'd be forced to be in each other's orbit again. I was trying to avoid him as much as possible until then. It was a tactic he knew well, which was why he kept signing me up for surgeries and animal checkups so I couldn't avoid him.

When I went on walks, he couldn't follow me. When I decided to take off and power-walk around the park, I could shut out the image of Greyson delivering nine little kittens that morning, could suppress the memory of him holding one so carefully in the palm of his hand that my stupid heart nearly burst. My god, it was like the weirdest kind of porn I had ever seen. I was instantly turned on and needed to get clear of the shared space as quickly as possible.

Thankful the weather was agreeable, the rain holding off for a while longer at least. I pulled my cell free, slowing my pace so Koda could rest. I dialed my sister, hoping she could help me get out of this funk.

"Finally ready to talk about it?" Selah asked right off the bat, still bitter about not being told why Greyson was there to help me babysit that night.

I rolled my eyes, tipping my head back. "Selah, nothing happened. We were having coffee when I realized I had to get to your house ASAP, he drove me and decided to stay. Literally nothing else is going on." I laughed, patting Koda's soft fur, wishing the white and silver coloring were a sleek jet black instead.

"Sure, and Bryan and I just went to dinner that night. We definitely didn't have mind-blowing sex after the kids went to bed," Selah deadpanned.

"Well did you?" I returned her blasé tone.

"Of course not. Those kids are constantly rotating in and out of our room. The only time we get mind-blowing sex is when they're all at school and we sneak in a quickie before we each have to go to work."

She wasn't wrong. I had stayed with my sister after each of her children's births, and through the years, one thing I'd realized was that privacy wasn't something to expect in a house full of small people. Between them and Selah, I could never pee or shower without someone barging into the bathroom. The locks had been taken off all the doors because my oldest nephew had once locked his little brother in the bathroom with a pair of scissors, telling him if he could cut his way out of there, he'd be considered for their super-secret brother club.

"I need a favor," I said, getting to the point, realizing how little time I had to make this call.

"What kind of favor?" Selah asked while my nephews screamed at each other in the background.

"The date kind of favor...I want a redo with Jonathan." I winced as the words left my mouth, but I was desperate—enough to consider douchebag Jonathan.

"Are you sure?" Selah asked, sounding concerned. She knew even without me saying anything that Jonathan was a dud. We weren't going anywhere.

"Yeah...do you think he'd want to go out with me again?"

"Kelly, don't be ridiculous—of course he asked Bryan if he could see you again, but Bryan said you might need some time because you're getting adjusted to your new job."

"I love that man." I sighed, thankful my brother-in-law was so considerate and had been quick to think of something to say to salvage my disastrous date.

"Me too. Now, I can set it up, but I think you guys need to go out alone," Selah muttered.

"Yeah, I think you're right." Maybe that was exactly the problem—maybe he had just been nervous. Maybe he didn't do first dates well...that was totally a thing.

"I'll have him text you, okay?"

"Okay, thank you, sis. Love you," I said, grateful for her help.

"Love you too. For the record, I think you're just wasting your time. We all know he'll never compare to the one who's holding the title in your head...and in your heart."

Yeah, that was exactly why I needed this date—to prove that there wasn't anyone holding a place in my life. Not anymore.

18

KELLY

It was Friday, the end of the longest week of my life. I had worked so hard to avoid Greyson that I was two seconds from hiding behind a coat rack and pulling a coat over my head so he wouldn't know I was in my office.

It was ridiculous. I had asked Jonathan if he'd want to go to dinner with me sometime, and he offered to take me out next week, which wasn't exactly what I'd had in mind. I needed a distraction, and maybe that made me a jerk. Probably did, but my past with Greyson was too much; it weighed heavy on me every day that he was near, and after seeing that video from Payton, I noticed her watching us interact more than normal. Same with the other volunteers.

I was glad for the weekend and for the reprieve from being around Greyson, although oddly enough, I hadn't seen him yet, and instead of feeling relieved, I just felt annoyed. Where was he? He had a surgery planned for noon, so I knew he had to come in at some point, but he was usually one of the first people into the shelter every day. Maybe he had a dentist appointment.

Maybe he was on a date?

No, he wouldn't do that…or would he? I blinked, trying to focus on what was going on. I could just text him. His number sat in my phone unused and regarded as if it were as deadly as a set of launch codes.

"Hey, Kelly, have you seen Greyson today? He isn't answering any of his emails, or his calls. His calendar says he should be in." Payton's light eyebrows pinched together in confusion as she spoke, and I could almost feel mine dip for the same reason.

Greyson was a meticulous planner, dependable to a fault, so when he said he'd be somewhere, he meant it.

"I haven't seen him yet, but I know he has a surgery at noon, so we will see him soon. Is it anything I can help with?" I offered, stepping closer to her desk. Payton was growing on me. Sure, she was too perky and way too happy on a regular basis, but she was sweet and she cared about these animals.

"It's just that Chance has a question about something and called asking if Greyson was in…I can just email him and tell him he's not. It's no big deal." Payton waved me off, returning her focus to her computer screen.

Why was Chance talking to Greyson without including me?

I didn't like that they seemed to be so buddy-buddy all of a sudden. Chance was a good guy, I knew that, and I knew he'd do anything for this shelter, but I was the director. Communications needed to go through me, right?

Trying to brush it off, I stormed toward my office and tried to get lost in paperwork until I could talk to Greyson about it myself.

Three hours later, Greyson still hadn't showed, nor had he called. His surgery time came and went, the poor dog rescheduled for later next week. Thankfully it wasn't a life-or-death situation, just a German Shepherd needing to be neutered.

"Hey Payton, I'm going to head out and see if I can't swing by Dr. Knox's just to make sure everything is okay." I dug through my purse, searching for my phone and bus card.

"Good idea. Do you want me to go with you?" Payton looked so hopeful that I'd accept her offer, but I needed to do this alone.

"Thank you, but it would help more if you could stay here and make sure everything runs smoothly." I smiled, reaching forward to grip her hand, showing I appreciated her.

"You got it, boss." She returned my smile and went back to her computer.

I tried to temper the nerves that rattled inside as the bus made it toward his side of town. It was only a short walk from the stop to his condo, but I couldn't get my hands to stop shaking.

What if something had happened to him? What if he was dead, and no one knew? I wouldn't have put it past his father to hire someone to kill him or something. That man was diabolical.

The weather was breezy, a rogue chill running down my spine as I walked from the bus stop down the street, toward Greyson's. The condos in this area were all brand new with gorgeous landscaping and creative design concepts. I loved tipping my head back, taking in all the new buildings that had been recently erected. Our town was growing, and with it, I felt like our little city was getting a facelift.

Finally, in front of his townhouse, I walked up the few steps and rapped my knuckles against the gunmetal grey door, hoping Grey didn't answer. Yes, I wanted him to be okay, but what if he was just taking a mental health day and wanted to be alone? I'd be mortified.

After a few seconds, no one answered, so I knocked again. I heard barking coming from inside, which was odd. The night I'd been there, there had been no dog, at least not that I knew of.

I could feel my face transform into a confused, twisted mess.

The dog came closer, barking as I knocked again. Still no Greyson.

Worried, I tried to turn the door handle. It was locked, but it had a keypad, likely for when he had packages delivered, or maybe when he just didn't want to take his keys.

Thinking back to my time with Greyson, I tried to think of what his code would be. He'd once given me his pin number to use his debit card, so I knew he liked using the combo 6778. Figuring it was worth a shot, I pushed in the digits and heard the door unlock.

He should probably, definitely change that.

Pushing the door open, I secured it behind me as the barking subsided.

"Greyson?" I yelled out, carefully treading into the space, appreciating it differently than I had when I was there the other night. Lighting fell gracefully over a nicely finished wood floor and the iron of the banister on the stairs. The kitchen was open with a massive gas stove range, an overhanging hood, quartz counters, a teal backsplash, and a farmhouse sink. It was cute.

Unfortunately, it was still slightly covered in unpacked boxes, but otherwise it was a beautiful space.

"Greyson!" I called again, and the dog, wherever it was, started barking again...somewhere from upstairs.

I turned and started to head up the steps, padding carefully, enjoying how new and modern the architecture was. I walked down the hall, hearing a dog whine behind a half opened door.

My heart was beating so fast I could hear it in my ears.

"Grey?" I whispered, pushing open his door. The room was dark, with a little light coming in from under his drawn shade. His large bed sat where it had the last time I was there, and Grey was in the middle, lying on his stomach with his face shoved into his pillow...unmoving.

I moved into the room, slipped off my high heels and jacket, and carefully placed my purse down against the wall. I walked closer to his side of the bed.

There on the little nightstand was some medication, and I carefully picked it up to inspect it: Theraflu, Alka-Seltzer flu tablets, ibuprofen, and Tylenol.

Oh no.

"Grey?" I whispered, pushing some of the blankets back—until a small yip from behind me startled me.

"Oh shit." I turned quickly, putting my hand on my heart.

There was a bundle of black fur lying on a large dog bed, wagging his tail while he kept his head down.

"Hey buddy, who are you?" I crouched closer while his tail thumped up and down excitedly. Finally, when I got within a foot or so of the dog, he jumped up and started licking my face.

Before I could regain my composure or even look clearly at the big dog, I heard a faint "Kat?" being called from the bed.

"Greyson?" I looked up, standing and walking toward his side of the bed again.

"You're here?" he rasped, sounding horrible and exhausted.

"Yeah, we all got worried when you didn't show for your surgery...you okay?"

He shifted to lie flat against his pillows while letting out a huff of air. "That was today? Shit."

He brought his hand to his forehead, revealing his muscled, tan forearms and his perfectly sculpted bicep. Memories of how good it had felt to be pressed up against that chest the other night ran through my head, winding down and spiraling into my gut, closer to the apex of my thighs.

"You're sick?" I asked, trying to redirect my thoughts and hopefully get the hell out of there.

"Yeah...happened kind of fast. Last night I just started feeling like shit...I took some pretty strong medicine, must have knocked me out pretty good," he mumbled, sounding sleepy.

Suddenly he sat up straight, our heads nearly colliding given how mine was lowered toward him.

"Sorry, I just remembered Jet—I haven't even let him out yet today...shit." He started to get up, but I pressed a hand to his chest. His skin was hot to the touch, clammy and obviously fevered.

"I'll take care of…" I stopped, what he'd said finally registering. "Did you say Jet?"

I flipped my head around to see the black bundle. In the darkened room, I couldn't make out any details, but it was the right size.

"Secret's out…yeah, I adopted him." Greyson gave me the sexiest side smile I had ever seen. My stomach dipped and my heart flipflopped around, like a fish caught in a fisherman's boat.

"You…you…" I couldn't wrap my brain around it.

"I knew you couldn't have him right now, but that doesn't mean you can't someday have him. I know you love him…I couldn't just let you lose him. So, I hired someone to front as my buyer and hold him for a few days until I could arrange for him to come stay here permanently."

His eyes searched mine, rimmed in red and tired, but curious.

"That is, until you're ready for him," he added softly, carefully moving his pointer finger to slide up to my wrist and back down my palm.

My throat was too tight, and tears stung the edges of my eyes.

"Greyson, that was…" I couldn't say it. I couldn't even speak it.

I wanted to run, wanted to hide from what this huge gesture and demonstration of kindness was doing to me, but an even bigger part of me didn't want to run at all.

I didn't want to go anywhere.

"Let me take him out and get him fed. I'll be back up in a little bit," I managed, the urge to cry slipping past my façade.

I kneeled in front of Jet, hugging him tight while those tears broke free, and then I walked him downstairs.

The dog food was in the mudroom, but from the looks of it, Jet had helped himself to whatever Grey had been eating for dinner the night before. Rice and chow mein were all over the hardwood floor. Thankfully, Greyson hadn't put down any rugs yet.

"Oh goodness, you poor thing," I said, moving toward the kitchen, seeing that Jet had already relieved himself inside the house. "Gosh, you were probably worried sick about him, huh bud?" I opened the back door to let Jet run out, filled his food dish, and checked his water. I cleaned up the mess he'd made then mopped and swept up the spilled food. Rummaging around under a few cabinets, I found a container of Clorox wipes and began wiping down all the surfaces and door handles.

The bark at the back door had me stopping and moving to let him in. It was so good to see him in the light of day. He was so handsome and happy. I knelt down, hugging him and wrapping my arms around his large body, holding tight as I contemplated how insanely lucky I was to have been given a second chance with him.

"I missed you so much, bud. I thought I had lost you forever," I whispered into his thick skin and glorious wrinkles. "I should have just adopted you myself. Screw the apartment—I'd rather live under a bridge with you than in that dumb place alone." Tears flowed down my face as the dog made some sound, cueing me to let him go. Standing, I swiped at my face. "Now, let's get your new daddy all cared for and healthy so he can take care of you."

I made some easy, Progresso chicken soup on the stove top, grabbed a sleeve of crackers and fresh water, and headed upstairs.

"Greyson?" I pushed the door open.

He was still in the middle of the bed, face down, but the blanket was pulled down to his waist, so his incredible, corded back was on full display.

I walked carefully over to his side with his lunch and set it down. "Grey, you need to sit up and try to get some fluids in you."

I sat on the edge of his bed, pushing some of his hair back; he was burning up.

"Grey, get up—you need to get in the shower," I said more forcefully. He didn't move, so I leaned forward and started pulling on him until he stirred.

"I'm fine, Kat. Thanks for stopping by," he slurred while yawning.

"Come on." I heaved while shoving my body under his side, hauling him toward the bathroom. He was in a pair of black boxers that dipped enough to show that perfect V cut.

"God, you're gorgeous." I huffed, knowing he wouldn't hear me, and even if he did, he wouldn't remember.

"Whaaatttt, you think I'm pretty?" he joked, slanting his head down until his lips were at my ear.

"Of course you're pretty," I said, helping him walk toward the tub so he could sit on the ledge while I got the shower going. "Sit here, I'm going to start this for you." I turned from him, toward the large, walk-in shower with stone tiling on every wall. "We need to get your fever down," I murmured, turning back toward him.

He was barely holding himself there on the ledge.

"Should be ready," I softly told him, taking in how glorious he looked, those sculpted thighs and six-pack abs, that strong neck with his mussed blond hair. He was too much on a good day, but like this—broken, sick—he could destroy me.

Greyson stood, holding himself steady with the wall. He shuffled closer to the shower until he was standing inside, but he hadn't reached the spray yet.

"Kat, I'm freezing. It hurts...I don't want to get under there, don't want to move. I just want to curl up in bed until it feels better." He looked back at me, pleading with me to let him.

Old me would have died for him right then and there if it meant he'd stop hurting, but the fever needed to come down. I wasn't the old me, but I did have a heart.

Knowing I might hate myself later, I stripped out of my clothes until I was just in my bra and underwear then stepped into the shower with him.

"Come on, Grey, you got this." I encouraged him to move under the spray, helping to direct him. "Just stand there. I don't need you to do anything but let the water hit your body."

Greyson gave me a curt nod. His broad shoulders, round with lean and corded muscle, tensed in discomfort. I crossed my arms, feeling awkward about watching the little rivulets of water flow down his body, and about how much that made me want to walk into his space, see if his arms would wrap around me.

"You're just going to stand there and watch?" Greyson's tired eyes lifted in question.

I smiled. "Unless you want me to leave? But you'll be really uncomfortable in wet briefs, and taking off wet briefs isn't the easiest thing, so let me help." I stepped forward and placed my hands on his hips.

"Whoa…wait," he said, low and raspy.

"What? I've seen everything before…" I lifted a brow at him, curious why he'd suddenly be shy with me. I was bullshitting him, and myself. I was too shy. It was me who was the coward regarding showers and nudity.

The smallest tick hitched itself along his mouth as he battled a smile. He looked horribly sick, but I could tell he was also curious how I'd react if he stripped. For the record, I had no freaking clue how I'd react.

He turned, stretching his arm out along the wall to hold himself up while narrowing his gaze on me.

"And you'd…what? Help me wash up?" He shuffled closer to the wall, closer to me.

I refused to shift backward or retreat from him. I was standing there, arms crossed, in my dark purple bra and black cotton underwear; it might as well have been a suit of armor.

I shifted forward half a step, a wicked smile on my face.

"If that's what you need, then yes, but be prepared, Greyson— I won't handle you very gently."

The water sprayed me in the face as it bounced off his rock-hard body. Not going to lie, it definitely made me feel less sexy and powerful having to wipe my face.

He began laughing, the sound oddly soothing given how I'd just tried to act with him. We both knew I was so full of shit.

He turned away from me, revealing his corded back with lines and grooves and all sorts of places for muscles to grow. Running his fingers through his hair, he ignored me as I stood behind him. I was cold, not being under the spray entirely but wet from the ricochet.

The longer he kept his back to me, the more stupid I felt. I was doing this to help him, but a teensy tiny part of me thought maybe he'd try something with me in here...I know how stupid that is, but the weak heart wants what the weak heart wants.

"Kat...if you take them off..." Greyson's voice sounded strained, like someone had used his vocal cords to rope a calf with a mound of dust and dirt flying all around. "I swear, I'll try to nail you...in here...against that shower wall, just like that time we went to Arizona."

My mouth was dry in an instant, remembering that weekend. We were supposed to be there for a wedding, but it was so fucking hot that we ended up not wanting to leave our hotel room for the entire weekend.

He fucked me against the shower wall so many times we joked about his sperm going down the drain and creating the next generation of ninja turtles. It was stupid. We were stupid, but it was also unforgettable.

"Oh" was all I managed to mutter while I waited for him to finish. The fantasy of him pinning me against the wall, pulling my bra cup down, and taking my hardened nipple into his mouth played in my mind like a dirty dream.

Would he grab my ass, pulling my thigh around him so he could enter me? Or would he get down on his knees, throw my leg over his shoulder, and feast on my pussy?

The ideas ran rampant in my mind, swirling like a pornographic cocktail. I swallowed, clenched my thighs together, and prayed for deliverance.

Greyson turned off the water and wiped the excess moisture from his face. He had goose bumps along his arms, and I could see him slightly shaking.

"Here, let me grab you a towel." I moved around him, careful not to touch him lest I explode from sexual tension.

I wiped my feet on his softer-than-hell bathmat and snagged two rolled towels from his thin closet space. I turned around, towel in hand, only to find Greyson sitting on the ledge of the tub, dripping wet, barely holding himself up.

"Kat, I feel like shit," he whispered, trying to let out a small laugh at the tail end, but all I heard was his teeth clattering together.

"Grey, shit, should I take you to the hospital?" I asked, wrapping the towel around his shoulders, rubbing his arms through the thick material.

He shook his head. "I just need some sleep."

"Try the soup first?" I asked, helping him stand.

"Yeah, okay...I think I need some dry boxers. Could you go grab them for me?" He looked up, those blue eyes so gentle and kind, unguarded.

Fuck me, I was done for.

"Yeah…where are they?" I turned, heading toward his room.

"Same as they always were," he called out from the bathroom.

"Right. So, top drawer," I said to myself, padding to his dresser half naked, half wet. I pulled open his top drawer and started digging around, pausing when I found an old photo.

It was of me. I had a huge smile on my face, I was wearing a thin tank top and a long flowy maxi skirt…and I was hugging Dutch, Greyson's dog.

It had been taken right after we started dating. He'd wanted to introduce me to his family but said they were all pricks, so instead he wanted me to meet Dutch, his only real family that mattered.

My stomach felt as though it'd dropped from out from under me. Why did he have a photo of me tucked away in his drawer? Although, it was of Dutch…so maybe it was the only photo he had and I just happened to be hugging Dutch in it?

"You get lost?" Greyson asked from behind me, his gruff voice wrapping around me like a velvet smooth blanket.

I turned, slowly, boxers in one hand, the photo in the other. "Sorry, I saw…" My eyes slowly rose, taking in the tight white towel wrapped around his waist. He was naked underneath, and the picture combined with him having Jet here…it was all just bubbling over into this new category we'd never been in before.

He reached forward, gently tugging the photograph from my hand, keeping his eyes on the picture instead of me.

"One of my favorites." He smiled and carefully put the picture down on the dresser then regarded me with that warm gaze.

"Can I have these?" He tugged on the boxer briefs in my hand, pulling them free with a tired smile.

"Right. Sorry." I realized the poor guy was sick and I was being ridiculous. I blinked, moved away from him and out into the hall, and shut his bedroom door behind me.

19

KELLY

GREYSON'S APARTMENT WAS SPOTLESS. I had scrubbed the dishes, mopped every surface, and even unpacked a few more of his boxes. His kitchen box had easy enough items to put away: a toaster, plates, cups—all things he could find after opening and closing a few cupboards.

I gave Jet a bath, drying him with Greyson's nice towels, then I let him snuggle with me on the couch while we watched a few classics. *The Breakfast Club* played in the background while Grey's gas fire flickered behind the glass, along the side wall.

I was wearing one of Greyson's old t-shirts with a pair of sweats that were too big, and if I moved around at all, they'd likely fall off. I was there to watch over Greyson, make sure he didn't die and all that, but I was also there to spend time with Jet. I had every intention of falling asleep on his crazy comfortable couch, with Jet, under a crazy comfy blanket, until I heard a loud thump from upstairs.

Jet made a sound, his brown eyes scanning over my way, like he was genuinely worried about his new owner.

Letting out a sigh, I gave in. "Fine, I'll go check on him."

I got untangled from the web of comfort I had tucked myself into and headed upstairs. After the shower and awkward boxer incident, I had mostly left Greyson alone. I'd waited thirty minutes before sneaking back in to ensure he was safely in bed and breathing, and it had been over three hours since.

I carefully pushed the door open and crept into the darkened room.

"Grey?"

I walked farther in, scanning for his imprint in the bed, hoping my eyes would adjust quickly to the dark. The day had waned, and although it wasn't super late yet, it was well into dinner time. I had told everyone Greyson was feeling under the weather but alive and that I was going to ensure he had someone set up to watch over him.

Julie had called and texted, which I ignored, knowing I'd have to face it the next day. But then Aubrey called, and I couldn't hold off any longer. Our conversation was friendly, upbeat, but took a turn when she flat-out asked me if I was taking care of Greyson.

I ended up spilling all the details to her about Greyson, our past, our issues. She felt horrible for letting him volunteer, for forcing me to work with him, but I reminded her that I needed this closure. She agreed but still felt inclined to remind me to nurture Greyson back to health so he could attend the charity function the following week.

"Greyson?" I whisper-yelled again.

A low moan met me from the floor, and I nearly tripped.

Bending low, I felt around, trying to gauge where his face was in the dark.

"Greyson, are you okay?" I asked, pulling carefully at the blankets entangling him.

"I need to take a piss and I'm all caught up in these fucking blankets," he responded, pain lacing his tone. I grappled with the fabric, stretching and pulling until I finally found the edge. Shoving down, I finally felt skin…hot, clammy skin.

"Oh Grey, you poor thing. You've still got this stupid fever." I ignored how my fingers dusted along the waistline of his boxers and reached for his hand. Helping him up, I aided him toward the bathroom while he held his stomach.

"Dammit, I fucking hate this." He groaned, leaning a hand against the wall, facing the toilet. I turned away to give him privacy, but I wouldn't be leaving him again. His fever seemed worse than it had before I forced him into the shower.

"You leaving?" he asked from behind me.

"Nope. Just get on with it. I don't want you to fall again."

He made some grunting noise before the sound of him pissing hit my ears. Some might have been put off by this seemingly awkward moment, but I'd helped Selah and Bryan potty-train those boys, and even now, when I went over there, they weren't shy about just pulling it out and peeing wherever they could— at the park, in the back yard. One time, the youngest, Jarrod, peed in Selah's sink, but I made all the boys swear to never tell her.

The toilet flushing had me turning back around. I gently grabbed his arm and led him to the tub.

"Grey, let me wash you down. You need to cool your body temp."

He grunted in response. Not exactly grateful for my nursing skills, was he?

I found a rag, wet it with cold water, and turned back toward the tub.

My stomach clenched at the sight of how defeated he looked. His golden hair was matted to the side, his face was ashen, and his mouth was drawn into a thin line of weariness. Carefully I walked to him, my purple painted toes meeting the edge of the tub, my knee grazing his. Thankfully, he let his head hang instead of looking up. If he watched me wash him down, it would be too much for me.

Starting at his forehead, I ran the rag gently across his skin, back through his hair, and down the back of his neck. His low groan nearly set me on fire from the inside out.

"That feels amazing, Kat."

I couldn't respond; instead I moved the cloth to his collarbone and carefully around his Adam's apple, down to his shoulders. More groaning emanated from Greyson, his eyes softly closed; it was a gorgeous display of utter vulnerability.

Wetting the rag again, I returned to Greyson, now wiping along the back of his shoulder blades and down his spine. The proximity nearly forced my chest to graze his face.

I let out a breathy apology, almost silent for fear of erupting into flames.

A strong hand gripped my hip as I continued my descent along Grey's smooth skin. My breath hitched at how hard his fingers dug into my waist.

I stopped mid-wipe, stepped back, and stared down, meeting a set of tired grey-blue eyes.

"This is mine," he whispered, toying with the hem of my shirt.

Silently, I stared down, my face flushing red. Why was I blushing? Why did it matter? He knew I had no clothes there besides my work attire.

Instead of responding, he tugged me closer to him by digging his fingers into the waist of the sweats rolled three times to stay on my hips.

"These too."

I was now standing directly in between his opened legs, staring down at him with no words on my tongue.

Heat tangled and twisted inside my entire frame, licking at my core, pummeling me in the chest. It was everywhere, suffocating me, betraying me.

"I like seeing you in my clothes," he rasped, keeping his fingers inside the seams of the sweats. He flirted with the band of my underwear, dipping his finger under and over it, twisting it around.

"I know you do" is what I whispered to the man who'd broken my heart, as if I'd done this on purpose. I hadn't. I wouldn't.

Still, I craved his eyes on me, his hands. I needed all of him.

"Why are you here, Kat?"

The air between us went dry, crackling with energy, like the atmosphere right before a thunderstorm.

"Because I care about you." I searched his eyes, which were now burning with lust.

"How much do you care?" Dark, delicious promise wrapped around his words, offering something I knew he shouldn't and couldn't deliver right now. He had a fever, he was sick...probably hallucinating at the moment.

When I didn't respond, his fingers splayed along my back, pulling me an inch closer.

"How much?" His voice tipped just enough to reflect raw openness. His eyes begged for an answer I wasn't ready to give. Even still, I toyed with the short strands of hair near his ear, skimming the shell. He closed his eyes as I carefully traced a line along his jaw and across his lips.

He made a guttural sound in the back of his throat as I marked his skin. I knew he wanted more. He wanted my lips, my tongue—but I couldn't, not when the real answer would be that I was at his house, taking care of him because I loved him. I was *in love* with him.

I couldn't tell him that. He'd retreat. He may have said he wanted me back, but I knew better than that. Greyson didn't know how to love people; he'd never been taught, and when we were together, I'd stupidly assumed I'd be that person to teach him about love.

I was wrong then, and I'd be an idiot now if I allowed myself the luxury of assuming he could love me back the way I loved him. As such, I put to memory the look on his face as my thumb traced his lip, right before I said, "I'm your friend, Greyson. I care about you as a friend."

He stiffened his shoulders, his eyes slowly opening with a sadness that nearly drove me to my knees. I couldn't be this close to him and see that expression, so I took a step back.

Then another.

"You need to eat something. I'm going to make you some soup after I straighten your bed. Unless...do you want to come downstairs and watch something with me and Jet?" Why did I sound so awkward? I had just shut down whatever Greyson assumed was going to happen here. I'd lied to the man, and now I was trying to see if he wanted to snuggle downstairs?

Greyson gave me the smallest nod with a weak smile.

"Sounds good. Thank you, Kat. Thanks for being here and for being my friend."

I returned his smile before turning around to leave. He was letting the friend comment settle, letting it exist between us. That's what I wanted, so why was there a burning sensation working its way up my throat and stinging my eyes? Why did it feel like Greyson had just declared that he didn't love me again?

20

GREYSON

"Hey, you're alive!" Payton excitedly yelled as I walked into the shelter. I returned her smile, but not her enthusiasm.

"Yeah, it was a little touch and go there for a little while," I joked, but honestly, I wasn't kidding. I had never been that sick in my entire life. It'd hit me out of the blue and taken me out faster than any other bug ever had. I would never have neglected Jet like I did, and I felt like total shit for that.

I was appreciative for Kat for so many reasons, the greatest of which was not telling me the condition my house was in when she got there. It had been two days since Kat left my side, after she declared I was healthy enough to recover on my own. She washed my bedding for me, cleaned my entire house, took care of Jet, and even made me a few meals. She was a fucking saint, yet all I could think about was how she'd said she was there because she was my friend.

The memory still felt like a shard of glass cutting into my chest. *My friend.*

I'd thought for some reason we were moving closer to being more than that. I knew she had been skittish after I tried to take her to dinner, but never in a million fucking years did I think that meant she was steering us toward the friend zone.

Dammit.

"You still look a little pale, though—you sure you're good to come back?" Payton sashayed around her desk, walking toward me with concern etched into her face. She was young, too young for me, but legal. I thought she was twenty or twenty-one, but I hadn't missed the billion and a half flirtatious remarks she'd made toward me, nor had I missed the number of awkward pictures she'd taken of me since I arrived.

She was nice enough, but immature and completely oblivious to how work relationships functioned.

"I'm fine, thank you. Is Kelly in?" I continued past her, toward the back of the building, where Kat's office was. I needed to start fixing this friend zone situation and ensure she knew how grateful I was that she'd taken care of me.

"Knock, knock." I rapped my knuckles along Kat's door before pushing it open.

Sitting at her desk, Kat was talking to someone on the phone, her head bent, that dark hair wrapped around her like a shield.

"Yes, well we're a strictly no-kill shelter unless there's a health reason the animal needs to be euthanized. I understand, and we appreciate any donation you'd be…right, yes, you can put it on your tax records." She nodded her head, still looking down at her notes. She hadn't even realized I was there.

Shit, based off the size of the pile sitting next to her and all the sticky notes that were out, along with highlighters and extra binders, it wasn't a good time to try to have that conversation.

Once she finally looked up, I smiled and gave her a little wave. She smiled back, giving me a quick glance of appreciation before her attention was yanked back to her conversation.

I pointed over my shoulder, silently saying goodbye before walking out.

I'd have to find her later to talk, because regardless of what she thought was going to happen between us, we would be talking, and it was time we got all the cards on the table. It was time for me to come clean about our past so we had a shot at a future.

"Hey, thanks for being willing to just chat with me alone." Chance smiled through the screen, rubbing his hand along the back of what looked like another goat—or maybe it was the same one...maybe they had an entire farm of goats? Who the fuck knew.

"No problem. I'm happy to help however I can." I leaned back, trying to appear relaxed and calm. Under my skin was an inferno of frustration burning and chafing my veins. Kat had been so busy that we hadn't had a chance to talk. She even had to cancel out on the surgery I'd scheduled her for. I showed up at her apartment with Chinese food and some flowers as a way of saying thank you, but she wasn't there.

Now, today, it was essentially a repeat of the previous day. Kat was already on the phone by the time I got in, she had already sent a memo about the surgery she likely wouldn't be able to help with, and now Chance needed to talk to me about the benefit dinner that was happening tonight. At least at the dinner, I'd have Kat all to myself. Images of dancing with her, pressing my palm into her spine while I spilled what I wanted us to become played out in my head, releasing some of the inferno, scorching me from within.

"I have a bit of an awkward question for you. I know it might be a little too personal, so I get it if you don't want to talk about it, but for the sake of the shelter, I wanted to ask. Aubrey doesn't even know about it yet, or else I think she might have tried to say something to Kelly already." Chance winced while the goat poked its head up, its mouth grazing the top of the table. "No, sit," Chance hissed. "Sorry, Pixy doesn't much like it when we talk on these computers."

I smiled, still not understanding this goat situation but finding it hilarious just the same.

"What kind of awkward question?" I laughed, trying to ease the discomfort out of my voice.

Chance's eyes bounced up from his pet back to me, on the screen. "Right...so there's this matter of Twitter."

Shit.

"Someone is saying she's your fiancée?" His raised eyebrow told me enough of what he was assuming about Tessa. Fuck, it was a miracle Kat hadn't seen any of the posts yet, but maybe Tessa had been making more of a fuss. Our YouTube channel hadn't been overly crazy recently. With me being sick and Kat being overloaded with work, there just hadn't been much to film, so why would Tessa still be banging on that drum?

"Sorry if I stepped on your toes, mate...just wanted to touch base without the ladies present," Chance said quietly, as though he didn't want Aubrey to hear. He stroked the goat's back and neck while he waited for me to answer.

I wanted to talk about that damn goat more than I did this topic; discussing it would take me back to losing Kat, back to my world being turned upside down.

"No need to apologize. I'm glad you asked...especially because, if you're seeing it out there, I'm sure others are too, and I know that can hurt whatever image people think they're getting with me and Kat." I ran my fingers through my hair while drawing in a shuddering breath. "The thing is, this whole situation is just one big clusterfuck. Tessa is an ex, someone I haven't talked to in any real regard for four years. We aren't seeing one another, and I think this is just a publicity stunt. She's trying to jump on our coattails to get followers and siphon off whatever fumes of this fame that she possibly can."

"Aw. Got it, mate. Sorry I brought it up." Chance winced, furrowing his sandy eyebrows.

"Don't be. I'm glad you asked. It's something I've been meaning to address for a while now." Josh had reminded me a few times, but he'd been busy with his own shit too, so I didn't blame him for not harassing me about it.

"Well, does Kelly know about it, or does she even care? Where are you guys at with all that?"

I laughed, hating how pathetic it sounded. "To be totally honest, I'm actually trying to win her back, but I'm having a shit time with it."

"Aw! That's actually something I'm well-versed in. Here's what you have to do." He leaned in closer, like he was conspiring with me. "You've got to do her landscaping." He winked.

Assuming it was a euphemism, I choked on a laugh. "Excuse me?" My eyes watered. What the hell kind of advice was that?

"No…no, no, that's not it. Get your mind out of the gutter." His Australian accent meant it came out as *gutta*, making me full-on laugh.

"Sorry, then what exactly do you mean? Because there's not even much to do in that department, if you know what I mean." I winked, trying to play whatever strange, fucked-up game we were playing.

"Christ, no." Chance shook his head, covering the goat's ears. "I was literally talking about landscaping—as in, go cut her lawn, trim her bushes, plant some flowers. Worked for Aubrey." He smiled like he'd just been dealt the winning hand of the longest, hardest round of world championship poker.

"Ah, well, I'm sure that would work, but she lives in an apartment."

"Well, fuck. Never mind, you're on your own." He laughed, joking with me, and it felt good to laugh about it with someone other than Josh. I returned his jest, reveling in the idea of winning Kat over with something as simple as pulling her weeds.

"I wish it were as simple as that, but our history is all muddled." I waved my hand, trying to dismiss it.

"Well then, un-muddle it." Chance gave me a curt nod, as if that was that.

It should have been that simple. I had envisioned it being that simple, but with all my plans for getting everything out on the table, I hadn't considered the hiccup of having Tessa out there spreading lies about us. It was just one more thing I'd have to talk about that could potentially distance us.

"What if that's not enough?" I hesitantly asked, not really sure why, but Chance had been forced to win Aubrey and it'd worked, so maybe there was hope for me.

"Then you just keep at it. You don't give up. It took me a long while to win Aubs over. I had to keep at it. So will you." His tone weighed heavy and serious, like a rock tied around my neck.

It had to be enough. She'd see it if I just put it all out there for her.

"Thank you, Chance. I appreciate the talk."

"No problem, mate. Have a good time at that benefit dinner." We gave each other a nod and disconnected the call.

I flipped my wrist over to see how much time there was before the benefit started. Two hours wouldn't be enough time, so it would have to happen at the actual event. I would tell her tonight and hope like hell it worked.

21

KELLY

THE LONG-STEMMED glass clutched in my fingers was starting to feel more like a weapon than a relaxing, bubbly drink of champagne. If I tossed it just right, I'd hit the redhead flirting with Greyson. She wasn't trying to hide it, either, regardless of the fact that we'd shown up together and he'd led me around the room by the small of my back, causing a riot of repressed emotions to crash to the surface.

Since leaving his house on Sunday, I'd been working to rid myself of these ever-growing sentiments. I'd known I was still in love with Greyson when we were nearly intimate, but how was it possible to continue to fall in love with the man? I had told him we were friends in his bathroom. I'd seen how his face fell, how his eyes turned down just the smallest bit and those lips I wanted to make my own had thinned. It bothered him. Whether he voiced it or not, I knew the truth.

Greyson had said he wanted me back, and at the time, I'd assumed that just meant physically, as though now that we were in the same vicinity, he'd want to just pick back up and be fuck buddies or something. That's what I assumed.

Like he'd forget our past, trying to brush it under the rug so he could just have his fun, regardless of how it would hurt me in the future.

But now…

Now, I wasn't so sure I had made the right call. I'd been wondering how to make my move and tell Greyson exactly how I was feeling ever since first stepping out of the limo that had been ordered for us.

My stomach had flipped as his scent closed in around me, reminding me that there had once been something there, something life-changing and unlike anything I'd ever felt in my entire life. Then Sienna showed up with her flawless thick red hair, hunter green dress, and creamy complexion. I immediately hated her when she pulled Greyson by the hand and feigned innocence.

As if someone doesn't know that they grabbed the hand of another person, someone's flesh and blood. You'd have to be a robot to miss something like that.

So, either she was artificial intelligence, or she was full of shit.

Greyson, thankfully, kept scanning the room, likely looking for me. I hoped he was looking for me, but maybe he was looking for a closet the two of them could sneak away to. He also frequently tried to disconnect from her every time she pawed at him or awkwardly turned to speak to someone while holding on to his forearm.

I hadn't stayed with them when she'd pulled him aside; I had other people to talk to, other faces to see and donations to secure. However, that was an hour ago, and now we were supposed to be seated next to each other, eating and talking to our tablemates. She still had him cornered, and at this rate, he'd starve by the end of the night.

I knew I had the worst resting bitch face that had ever been, but Sienna needed to know that I didn't approve of her stealing my date. I didn't approve of her obvious boob job, or the extensions she may or may not have had.

But it didn't matter what I approved of or not; Greyson was still over there talking to her.

Sienna leaned in to whisper something in Greyson's ear, and a heart-stopping grin transformed his features, making mine putter out in return. If there hadn't been a speech we were required to do together, I'd have left. Instead, I let out a sigh, stood, and headed for the restroom. I just needed to walk and think, get my eyes off the fucking redhead.

My high heels clacked along the floor as I made my way toward the restroom, the gleaming white flooring under my feet meeting my gaze as my eyes refused to lift to the mirror. I didn't want to face the person I'd become tonight. I had only ever really been jealous one other time in my life, and that was when Tessa walked out with Greyson. Seeing him with Sienna was making all those demons come back out, and I hated it.

Reluctantly, I raised my head, fixing my glare on the black, strapless dress that snugly hugged my frame. My hair was fastened in a way that half was pinned up, the other half hanging in sleek strands against my back. I liked how I looked, but I couldn't stop the freight train of thoughts as I compared my clammy pallor to Sienna's creamy perfection.

I hated that my mind went there, but I'd have been a liar if I didn't allow myself the honesty of how painful it felt. Footsteps clicked along the floor, announcing someone's arrival, and I made quick work of fixing my makeup then turned to leave.

Once I was outside the bathroom, a strong hand landed on my elbow, tugging me to a stop.

"Kat," Greyson's husky voice rasped in my ear.

He stood against my back, so close I could feel every hard line and delicious groove.

"Greyson," I replied coolly, like I didn't care and hadn't noticed that he had been flirting all night.

"We need to talk."

I pulled away, attempting to walk ahead of him and break the magnetic touch. His arm banded around me a second later with a low growl coming from the back of his throat.

"I'm serious. I need to talk to you."

"Greyson," I warned, tilting my head to the side. "You've had all night to talk to me. Now isn't the time."

I hated being the one to bring up Sienna, but if he was going to try to spin a tale around wanting to talk to me then he was delusional.

"Shit. Kat, that's not what..." He trailed off as an elderly woman wearing a long, flowy green dress hustled toward us.

"There you two are!" She held her palms out as she approached. "Come now, they're about to start the speech, and we are planning on having you both go up to accept the check." She moved behind Greyson, who'd stepped to my side, and began herding us toward the entrance of the hall.

I looked up in time to see Greyson's eyes narrowing on me with a look that said he promised to catch me later. Fat chance.

We entered the room as a tall man in a tailored suit began talking about the importance of having a place for these poor animals to go. He listed off statistics and a few other numbers while the woman in the green dress kept Greyson and me in place, like we were schoolchildren.

Finally, the man turned to his right, waving us onto the stage.

The room erupted in cheers, which had my mind flayed wide open. Why on earth did these people care this much? I was a no one, someone keeping their head down until my next job, whatever that might be. I had stopped living for my dream job, stopped caring about law and becoming a lawyer. I wasn't willing to leave Selah, and I was blacklisted from the firms here in Temecula. Greyson had seen to that.

The man of the hour stood too close for my comfort while we waited for the tall man to get on with what it was we were doing up on the stage.

"We'd like to present the Park Avenue Animal Shelter with this generous donation of fifty thousand dollars in honor of working to protect the animals of our city. We recognize the work you've put in to offer your services for free, Dr. Knox, and have been so moved to live out that same example of generosity."

A massive rectangular check made its way up the stairs toward the left. Sienna walked forward carrying it, smiling wide like this was her moment, not ours. My heart sank as Greyson accepted the check from her hands, grazing her fingers in the process. She nearly tried to shove me out of the way as she maneuvered for a place at the podium.

Greyson used his free hand to grip my waist to keep me rooted next to him, but there was no missing how awkward it was. Face on fire, I tried like hell to ignore how uncomfortable I felt. I knew it was an entirely different situation, but somehow it felt like I was back in that room where Greyson had walked out with Tessa, where he'd humiliated me in front of everyone. What if Greyson had only been joking about wanting to get back together? What if Sienna was his girlfriend and in on the prank?

My stomach soured at the idea.

I tried to push those thoughts away as the room cheered for us. I missed the speech Greyson made; it was something about how grateful he was for the shelter and the opportunity to work with me. My heart felt like it was made of wood: old, warped, and splintering into tiny, irreparable pieces.

I needed to get out of there. I tried to wiggle free of his hold because of how close Sienna was standing to both of us. I needed air, room, a place to breathe and rid myself of all these emotions that had flared to life. My eyes flitted up, scanning the crowd, not for any other reason but to locate an exit. There along the side of the stage was Greyson's camera crew, all set up, filming us. I wondered if they'd caught him talking to Sienna all night, if they'd been annoyed to not get their star couple in the shots they wanted.

That was probably why Greyson was gripping my waist, probably why he'd wanted to talk outside the bathrooms before. He likely realized his massive fuckup in the filming department and was desperate to fix it before the night was through.

Finally, the older gentleman clapped, along with the room, excusing us to leave.

Thank God.

As soon as Greyson's hold let up, I darted toward the edge of the stage, leaving him behind to deal with the woman in the green dress and Sienna. I didn't care how he ended his evening, or with whom.

I was going home.

I took the limo that was secured for Greyson and me and didn't feel an ounce of guilt in doing so. I had the driver drop me at my sister's, only to find out one of her kids had the flu. She wouldn't let me in to help her, regardless of how much I swore I could handle it.

Memories of Greyson sleeping in my lap after we watched Netflix together down on his couch flashed in my mind. I'd been there for him because I loved him. I cared. Fucking hell, I still cared, and I still loved the idiot. The problem was, I couldn't seem to separate loving him and being in love with him.

Loving him meant I could do what was best for him from afar, not being a crazy ex-girlfriend, showing up at his house unexpectedly, not drunk calling or texting him...those kinds of things. However, now...the lines were blurring. I had never stopped loving him, but after a while, I had fallen out of love with him, into hurt and blame...all those sorts of unhealthy things.

The longer I was in that limo, the more time I had to debate what sorts of things I had rolling around in my head. Anger, unaddressed hurt that had festered and blistered my heart, never fully healing. Devastation I'd never gotten answers for. Humiliation I'd never earned.

Suddenly, I needed to know exactly why Greyson had done all those things all those years ago. I had told myself over and over that it didn't matter, that it was better left in the past—that *he* was better left in the past. But not anymore, not when my mind had already convinced itself that Greyson had planned something similar with Sienna. So, I had the driver take me to Greyson's house.

Tonight, I was getting the full story of why Greyson Knox dumped me and wrecked my heart beyond repair.

22

GREYSON

Fuck.

Fuckity-fucking-fuck.

The night didn't go how I'd planned. Not even close.

From the moment we arrived at this benefit, I was supposed to be glued to Kat's side. Drinking champagne with her, dancing with her, slowly grazing her backside, tantalizing her into a kiss. We were supposed to talk about Tessa, about that night four years earlier…about it all.

Then Sienna showed up.

Sienna was an old family friend. Her father knew my father, and they went way back, so I knew she'd want some of my time. I figured I'd smile, nod along with the 'remember when' stories she always had on hand, and then sneak back to my date.

What I hadn't expected was Sienna to have information about Tessa.

Information I desperately craved and needed in order to straighten out this massive clusterfuck.

So, I stayed next to her, waiting in and out of random greetings and conversations just so I could find out all the details Sienna knew. Unfortunately for me, there were quite a few interruptions, side conversations, and opportunities for Sienna to abuse her time by introducing me to different people. I glanced at Kat several times throughout the night, gauging how she was doing, but every time I saw her, I felt like I would die from exposure on the spot.

Pure ice was coming from her cold stares, aimed at me, Sienna, and anyone who dared walk up to speak to us.

Worry knotted in my stomach over what she might think, and panic set in when she darted for the bathroom, a mere three minutes after Sienna finally finished spilling the story about Tessa.

The night wasn't supposed to end with Kat taking off in our limo by herself to God knows where. Once I finally secured an Uber, I went to her apartment building and waited outside in the hallway for almost thirty minutes before the nosey next-door neighbor finally told me she hadn't been home.

Next I went to her sister's, only to find that she'd sent Kat on her way due to the same epidemic that had taken me out the weekend prior. Now, I was riding back toward my side of town in my second Uber of the night, worried sick over where Kat had gone.

Once the car pulled up to my house, I lagged going up my stairs, feeling sullen and frustrated. I pulled my cell free, checking to see if maybe Kat had texted, or if I'd missed a call. *Nothing.*

Stepping up to my door, I punched in the keycode on the keypad and pulled on the handle. The lights in the living room were on low, the television blared *The Big Bang Theory*, and on my couch was Kat, dressed in one of my t-shirts, a blanket covering her lap.

Jet's head rose from the blanket at my entrance, but Kat didn't spare me a glance. She continued eating from the bag of pretzels that sat behind Jet's back.

I shut and locked the door, toed off my shoes, and peeled off my suit jacket as I walked past my foyer farther into the house.

My stomach dipped with excited energy at seeing Kat resting on my couch, in my shirt, petting my dog. I mean, Jet was mostly hers—I'd only adopted him for her—but still.

She was in my space, and fuck if it didn't feel like she was sending me a message, marking her territory or something, especially after the shitshow with Sienna.

I carefully padded across the living room until I was gently folding into one of the armchairs, opposite the couch, my eyes never leaving Kat's face. I watched in wonder as tiny strands of her hair fell around her face, all soft and silky perfection. My fingers itched to push them behind her ear so I could see her face without interruption.

She had the most beautiful face. Her blue eyes always glittered with green and gold flecks, and her bottom lip was luscious and full, framed perfectly by her bow-like top lip, making it look as though she always had a secret she was keeping.

I used to love tracing her lips with my fingers, pulling the bottom one down just the smallest bit, covering it with my mouth.

"Greyson, your staring is too loud," Kat said sarcastically, not looking over at me.

I smiled, stretched my legs out, and sank into the chair. "So, you remembered my code, huh?" I shouldn't have been surprised. I figured she'd remembered when she showed up the previous weekend, but I needed some way to address the fact that she was here in my apartment.

"Yep, I still remember." She let the P pop.

"I went to your apartment." I watched her, resting my chin on my fist, waiting to see what direction she wanted to take this in.

"I bet you did," she muttered. More sarcasm.

"Then I went to Selah's," I continued, watching her facial expression carefully. Her eyes bounced quickly over to me then back to the television. "Sucks about the flu situation," I added, baiting her.

"Yep," she quipped.

Heaving a sigh, I got up, walked over, and crouched down in front of her.

"But you came here." Not a question, just a confirmation.

Her eyes finally drifted to mine, the look in them feeling like a punch to the gut.

She set the remote to the side and slid forward until she was on the edge of the couch. Realizing his resting spot was shifting, Jet moved his head to the couch instead of her lap. The blanket rose, revealing creamy skin. Under my shirt, she wasn't wearing anything but a black scrap of underwear.

Fuck.

I inhaled sharply, my hands automatically going to the space next to her legs. She continued forward until her palms rested on my shoulders and her legs caged me in along my torso. The warmth was incredible, a shot of electricity shooting across my shoulders and along my sides at her proximity.

"There are some things we need to talk about," she whispered, husky and flirtatious.

I swallowed, not daring to tear my gaze from hers. "We do."

She nodded again, tugging at my bowtie.

My hands went to her thighs, running my palms up her silky soft skin, desperate to hold the fear I had of her bolting any second now at bay.

I wanted her to hear me out. I *needed* her to hear me out.

"Kat, there's something I need to tell you," I murmured, while she worked on unbuttoning my shirt.

Using the collar, she tugged me closer, plastering those delicious lips against mine. Soft yet hard, she was perfect as she slanted her head to the side, deepening the kiss. Groaning, I moved my hands up her rib cage, palming her bare breasts.

"We can talk later, I guess," I muttered against her mouth.

"Mmmmm," she responded, smiling against my lips. "Greyson?" she asked, pulling away for a brief second. "I don't want to talk about tonight. Not yet."

She returned her mouth to mine, moving her hips closer to my chest, moving her core forward as she did. Leaning up, I pushed her back into the couch, her arms going around my neck as I gripped her by the ass and pulled her up.

Her legs wrapped around my waist, holding tight while she moved her lips to my neck, kissing my Adam's apple, then lower. I flexed my fingers on her ass, loving the smooth feel, remembering how good it felt to have her like this, in my arms...in my bed.

Pushing open my bedroom door with my shoulder, I walked in and carefully laid Kat down, staring at how my shirt had risen enough to show her stomach, her thong, her legs...all of her.

"Greyson, we're going to talk tonight, and I don't care if you don't want to give me the answers. You're going to fuck me, then answer me. Do you understand?" she asked, sitting up, pulling the shirt over her head.

I smiled at her demand while I finished unbuttoning my shirt.

"You got it," I promised, moving my fingers to my pants, but then she stopped me.

"No. Let me." She sat up, shifting on her knees toward me, the soft glow from downstairs leaking in through the open door, providing the only light in the room. I wanted to see more of her, but I wasn't about to stop her fingers from working on my slacks, briefly brushing against my hard-on.

Her fingers worked my pants until they were free, sliding down my legs. I took both feet out, standing there in my boxers. She stared at me, carefully tracing my pectoral muscle with her delicate finger, trailing down until she got to the elastic at my hips.

Leaning forward, she pressed her lips to my skin, landing kisses gently and softly along my chest. It was like a memory someone found, lost and forgotten, opening it and allowing me to see inside. Utter perfection.

"Greyson," she whispered against my skin. A plea...but not to touch her; this was something deeper. She pushed her fingers up into my hair, tugging on the longer strands.

I gripped her waist, desperate to dig into her skin and sink into her heat.

"I don't want you to be gentle with me tonight. I want you to be as ruthless with my body as you have been with my heart. It'll make it easier." She pressed a gentle kiss to my lower lip, only to bite it a second later.

My sexual past with Kat was riddled with every kind of preference from sweet and slow, half our clothes on, to scathing hot, rough and dirty. We never had any inhibitions in what we did, no guilt, no shame. I remembered one time in particular when I put my leather belt in between her teeth, telling her to bite down while I fucked her from behind, slapping, leaving angry welts on her ass. She came hard, fast. She liked it rough, and I always fucking loved that she trusted me with that part of our relationship.

But tonight...her words landed in all the wrong places. Instead of lighting me on fire, dousing me in lust, I felt shattered.

Be as ruthless with my body as you have been with my heart.

It'll make it easier.

What was she talking about? What the hell did she plan on discussing with me?

"Kat, baby...take a second...just wait." I pushed her shoulders, and she took the opportunity to reach for my length inside my boxers. "Hang on, let's just wait a minute." I sat down next to her.

"Grey, this isn't going to be a fun night for me, so I'd appreciate it if you could at least give me an orgasm for my heartache," she chided, brushing a hand over my chest.

"What are you talking about?" I asked, still so confused.

She let out a sigh. "I don't want to talk about it until I get a well-deserved orgasm. Trust me, once we start talking, we won't be in the mood to bang each other's brains out."

"I'm not going to be ruthless with you—"

"Please, Grey," she begged. "Please, I need it tonight. It's stronger and better than any shot I could throw back."

"But, I'm not—" I tried again, only to have her put a finger up to my lips.

"The sooner we fuck, the sooner we can talk."

Why was she adamant about this? My heart sank at her refusal, but if this was what she really wanted... "Okay."

"Thank you," she whispered. "Don't hold back. I want all of you, as hard as you can give me."

She sat back, waiting for me to make the move. My movements felt forced, robotic, not because I didn't want this woman, but because I loved her and I needed her to have that reassurance before we ventured into this kind of physical intimacy.

Pushing past my mental reservations, I ran my hands up her thighs, resting them at her hips, gently tugging on the material covering her there.

"Take these off," I requested softly.

She did as I said, keeping her eyes on me, still leaning back against the mattress, supporting herself with her elbow propped up. She slid the black piece down her legs, kicking them to the side. My eyes, adjusting to the limited light, took her in. Her smooth skin, her bare entrance, her *perfection*.

I barely brushed the pad of my thumb against her mound, her eyes tracking my every movement. I wanted a picture of her like this, ready and desperate for me to wreck her.

Wrapping my fingers around her hips, I pushed my thumbs into the space next to her smooth entrance and pulled her closer to the edge of the bed.

"Get on all fours and face the wall," I instructed through gritted teeth, my voice heavy with need.

She did as I said, slowly getting up, turning until her ass was facing me.

I ran a hand through my hair, torn on what to do. It was what she wanted, but fuck, we needed to have the longest conversation ever after this.

Dropping my boxers, I stepped closer to the bed, remembering how much I loved her like this—open and ready for me.

"Are you wet?" I asked roughly, already feeling the strain in my voice from how hard I wanted to fuck her.

"Soaked," she whispered back.

"For me?" I slowly pushed the pad of my thumb into her ass cheek.

"Only for you."

Shit, I hadn't even touched her slick entrance yet and I wanted to come. I raised my other hand, pressing my thumb into the opposite ass cheek.

Pulling them apart, I spread her open, and instead of pressing into that tiny hole with my finger like I'd done in the past, I hoped to surprise her by pressing my tongue there.

As I shoved my face into her crack and my tongue as far into that tight bundle of nerves as I could possibly go, she gasped, following it with a raspy "Fuuuucckkkkk."

Lifting my face, I smiled, asking, "Do you want more?"

"Yes, Grey, more please," she whined, rocking her ass back and forth.

I loved that she didn't know what I was doing to her next, loved the thrill of her reaction to whatever it was going to be.

Carefully brushing my fingers up and down her perfect globes, I repeated the gentle touch a few more times before slapping her there. The loud thwack echoed in the room, along with her hiss and throaty "Yes, oh my god, yes."

I repeated the action on her other cheek, wishing I could see the usual bounce that accompanied her rear when I smacked her there.

Walking toward the side of the bed, I clicked the lamp on, illuminating the room with a soft glow. She was beautiful, waiting for me to touch her, waiting for me to ruin her.

Her head popped up in surprise. I took advantage, stepping closer, pushing her hair back.

"I need to see you." For a second, I was caught in reverence with how beautiful she looked, those sharp green eyes, dark brows at ease, no worry on that beautiful face of hers. The desire to hold her, to be gentle was right there in my chest, begging me to make her whole...but I knew she needed this other side of me tonight, and I wanted to give it to her.

Blinking back my concern, I shoved my finger into her mouth and demanded, "Suck."

She moved slowly, her eyes staying glued to mine while she lapped my finger, swirling her tongue over the tip. I gripped my length, stroking it up and down in rhythm with her flow.

"Is that what you'd do to me? Would you wrap those full lips around my cock and suck?" I asked, voice husky and aroused.

She reached up, gripping my fist, pushing my digit farther into her mouth at my filthy question. She loved the dirty talk, and I loved letting myself go and saying every obscene thing that popped into my head.

"You're so fucking wet for me, aren't you?" I stroked my length harder, rolling the precum around the tip. "Look down." I held my cock in my firm grip, squeezing the base.

Her eyes dropped to the clear fluid beading at the crown.

"Clean it up." I forced her head down. I'd long ago let go of the apprehension associated with feeling like I was disrespecting her. Every person had their own kink, the thing that aroused them, that got them to catch fire. Me being a dominant asshole in the bedroom was hers.

Her lips wrapped around the top, licking the tip, bringing her eyes up to meet mine. "Mmmmm, so good."

"Such a dirty mouth," I muttered, pulling her chin up, slamming my mouth hard against hers. I kissed her, invading her with my tongue, relishing the taste of her.

Finally, I pulled my lips free and reached to pinch her nipple. "Show me how wet you are." I stroked my shaft, up and down while she reached in between her legs, bringing her fingers up. They glistened in the low glow of the room.

I bent down, grabbing her wrist, and I sucked the wetness from her fingers into my mouth, groaning as I licked her clean.

"Fucking perfect."

I let her go, moving back to her ass. I leaned in and licked her wetness from her folds, dragging my tongue up to her asshole. She moaned in response, rocking back toward my face.

"You want more, baby?" I asked, pushing a finger into her wet hole, rubbing around the rim.

"Oh my god, Grey."

I reached down, grabbing her pussy, shoving two fingers into her slick heat. Loving how it sounded, I slid the wetness up, smearing it along her crack.

I leaned down, pulling her pussy into my mouth, sucking and licking her wetness. I was relentless, not letting up, bringing her to the brink of orgasm only to withdraw and slap her ass.

"Greyson!" she cried out, demanding I return to her.

"Are you aching for me?" I gently shoved two fingers into her, rubbing and gliding my finger along her slit.

"Grey, I need you to fuck me," she begged. I loved when she begged.

"Get up." I slapped her ass one last time, hard enough to warrant a hiss.

She crawled up, getting into a sitting position.

"Get on the floor, sit on your knees." I stroked my dick as her perfect tits bounced. She grabbed them, rolling the rosy buds between her fingers.

I sat on the edge of the bed, watching as she got on her knees before me.

I didn't want to do this tonight, but it was a big part of the rough sex that she loved.

Standing from the bed, I looked down at her, loving how desperate she looked, how fucking wrecked she already was.

"Open your mouth." I grabbed the back of her head while she kept her eyes on me, opening up for me.

Leaning forward, I shoved my dick inside her mouth, rough and crass.

She immediately wrapped her lips around the tip, gripping the base with her hand. Scooting forward, she waited for my command.

"Suck." I shoved my hips forward, nearly choking her with my length, but she made room for me, licking and sucking, gaining the upper hand with her quick movements.

"Fuck, baby. Yes." I moaned while she sucked me off, swirling her tongue around the tip, devouring it a second later. Her eyes were so big, round, and perfect, and her free hand rested on her tit, rolling the nipple and squeezing.

I rocked inside her, fucking her mouth, loving how she kept nearly gagging only to recover and take me deeper. My fingers tugged on her hair, pulling on the silky strands as I shoved my hips forward.

She gripped my ass, bringing me so close, closer, sucking harder. *Shit.*

Quickly, I pulled out, not ready to come yet.

I sat down on the edge of the bed and looked down at her, loving how she wiped at the edges of her mouth.

"Straddle me," I commanded gruffly.

She slowly stood in front of me, teasing me, holding her breasts together, pinching her nipples.

"Condom?" she finally asked, raising an eyebrow.

"I haven't fucked anything other than my hand in four years, Kat. You were my last, and as far as I'm concerned, you'll be my only. If I could come inside you, guaranteeing me a baby, sign me the fuck up."

Her eyes glittered with something, softening and nearly crumbling. I wanted to pull her into my arms and lay it all out, have that conversation, tell her what she meant to me once and for all, but she slammed her eyes shut, closing off her emotions.

Gripping my shoulders, she climbed into my lap, but not on top of my dick. Instead she began rubbing her pussy against my length.

"Fuck," I hissed, loving how wet and hot she was for me. She rocked back and forth, not letting me enter her.

"Grey, I love how good you feel," she teased, knowing it'd rile me up because she always said that when I was inside her, not against her.

I gripped her waist, pulling her forward, helping set the rhythm. Her breaths shortened, becoming more and more shallow as she increased her tempo.

"Is this how you want to come? Humping the shaft of my dick instead of having it inside you?"

Her breathing was labored as she opened her eyes. "Grab a condom then," she challenged.

"You wanted me to ruin you," I reminded her gruffly.

I stood up quickly, realizing we would need to do this another way. Grabbing her wrist, I pulled her across the room. Stopping by a random tie lying on the floor, I joined her wrists and tied them together, tying the end off on the hook that held my heavy curtains.

The length raised her arms above her head, removing her ability to fight me.

"Do you really care about the condom?" I asked, lowering to the floor, my eyes level with her slick pussy. I gripped her hips, waiting for a response; she only stared back at me. To encourage her along, I stuck my finger into her heat, nice and slow, then lowered my mouth, licking along her folds.

Her hips bucked while she moaned out, "No."

"Are you sure?" I asked again, adding a finger, swiping my tongue in and out, pulling her clit into my mouth.

"Greyson, fuck me—with or without the freaking condom." She writhed against the restraints.

I stood, pushing the tip of my cock into her wetness, dragging it along her slit, up and down, but not going any deeper.

She pushed her hips forward, trying to find purchase.

"*Tsk-tsk*, not yet."

I pulled her nipple into my mouth, massaging her breast while moving my dick along her wet center, torturing her.

"You're so fucking wet, baby," I rasped in her ear, licking the sensitive lobe there. "Do you want my cock inside you?"

"Please," she whimpered, her arms shaking.

I moved behind her, separated her ass cheeks, and lined my dick up with the opening of her pussy.

I shoved inside, hard and fast.

"Fuccccccckkkk," Kat moaned, pushing back against me.

I stabilized her hips, pulling out and shoving in again, harder this time. This angle wasn't enough, but it would suffice for the teasing I planned to do.

With my dick inside her, I reached around her and played with her clit, barely moving.

Kat let out a moan that quickly turned into an agitated growl.

"More, Grey. I need more."

"So do I." I reached up, untying her from the hook and releasing her hands, only to bind them once more behind her back. Keeping my hand on her ass, squeezing, I walked her to the bed and pushed her face into the comforter. I grabbed the tie that bound her wrists, loving how it looked to have them together directly above her round ass. I ran my hand down her back, dipping my fingers around to her clit before lining up with her entrance.

"Are you ready for me?" I grunted, massaging her folds. So slick, so wet, *so mine.*

"I don't want it to matter if I am or not. Ruin me, Grey," she said, needy, nearly pleading.

I shoved inside her as hard as I could while pulling on her bound wrists. I didn't give her a chance to adjust before pulling out and shoving back in harder, going deeper.

I repeated the process, pulling out almost entirely then shoving back in with a loud smack of our skin slapping together. Once my shaft was coated entirely in her arousal, I began pumping faster.

"Fuck. Fuck. Fuck." She moaned repeatedly as I viciously pummeled into her, gripping the bind that kept her hands restrained.

I was about to come, so I slowed us down, taking a second to admire how good the red handprints looked on her skin, especially with my dick inside her. Smiling, I gently smacked her ass while slowly rocking into her.

"Harder, Grey." She groaned loudly. Shit, I missed how loudly she used to yell for me.

I slapped her harder then returned my hands to her hips, viciously fucking her with more force than before.

"Oh my god! I'm...I'm...oh gooooooodddddddddd." She moaned so loud and clenched so tight, my release following hers while I emptied myself inside her.

"Fuck, Kat. Fuck!"

Spent, I leaned forward, breathing hard, glistening with sweat. I carefully pulled out, gently untied Kat's hands, and headed toward the bathroom. Once I pulled on a pair of sweats, I walked back to Kat with a warm rag and helped her clean between her legs, lightly brushing away the strands of hair stuck to her face.

"Thank you," she said meekly, handing the rag back to me.

I tossed it in the hamper and crawled into bed.

"What about Jet?" she asked, joining me under the blankets.

"He'll wander up here when he's ready," I said, pulling her to my chest. "Now...we've done what you wanted, so let's have that conversation you promised me." I kissed the top of her head.

She let out a heavy sigh and turned in my arms until she was facing me. "I want to know what happened that night...when you walked out with Tessa, announcing your engagement. I want to know what I did wrong." Her voice caught on the last word, and it felt like she'd shot me in the heart with a dull arrow.

Is that what she still thought? How could I have allowed her to carry around that assumption for so long?

"Kat, shit...no, it was all so messed up," I started, pulling her even closer, hoping she'd find some way to forgive me. "Remember that week, how I'd been hinting at the engagement? That was the entire reason our families were going to go in on that deal together. I had every intention of announcing *our* engagement that night."

"Then what happened?"

"My father happened." I let out a sigh so heavy it should have crushed us both. I'd believed him, and I had doubted Kat, ruining us.

"What did he do?" Kat whispered into my chest, likely as terrified to hear the truth as I was to tell it.

"He lied to me. Showed up with these pictures...proof that you'd been cheating on me. I was devastated. What's worse, he said you'd slept with Andrew Parker—do you remember him?" I tilted my head just the slightest bit to try to gauge her reaction, not that it mattered. Andrew had confirmed on his own that nothing had happened between them, said it was all bullshit.

"I do. He was nice to me, gave me a seat at one of the tables during one of the stupid parties Tessa threw that you wanted to attend."

I cringed at the memory. I'd gotten drunk and left Kat in the house while I went outside on the beach, night surfing and being an absolute moron. I could have died, something could have happened to her…I was such a fuckup back then.

"I'm sorry, Kat. I'm so sorry for that night and for the other nights when I let you down. I was so blown away by you, by your brain and your heart, the fact that you were down to earth, wearing hoodies and jean shorts when every other girl only wore Fendi and Prada, sipping on White Claws while watching everyone live life. You actually lived it, and it both terrified and enthralled me."

"So, you believed your dad?" she asked, barely above a whisper.

I felt a knot forming in my chest, in my throat…the confession right on the tip of my tongue, ready to damn me to hell and throw away what could have been.

"I did. I was so hurt that I just wanted to hurt you back, so I thought up the idea with Tessa…it was all fake. You were the real one. You were the only thing that was real out of all that. I just…" I searched for the right words. "I just wanted you to hurt like I was hurting."

"How come you never came after me?" Kat's voice hitched, sounding strained, like she was holding in a sob.

"You'd left for Europe when I found out. I called, but you must have changed your number or blocked me or something, and it wasn't something I was about to drop into your DMs. I wanted to talk to you, but I had no idea when you would be back, so I changed course…went to UC Davis and waited."

"You waited?" she deadpanned, like she was trying to turn over the idea and it wasn't sticking.

"I waited four years, not knowing what happened to you or where you went—until one day when I saw a local news clip about you taking over the animal shelter. I knew it was my chance. Most shelters don't have on-call vets, but I put in a call to my mentor, Dr. Santé, just to see if he'd be willing to cover me. Once I got his blessing, I called Chance and Aubrey, asking if they'd make an exception. I did it only for you, to get you back."

My admission hung in the silence between us, and I waited for her body to disconnect from mine, her leg to unwind from my calf, her breath to leave my space...but nothing happened. She didn't move. She didn't do anything but snuggle closer.

"I love you, Greyson. I'm still in love with you, and whatever damage was done in our past, I promise not to carry it into our future as long you don't."

Then she kissed my chin and might as well have physically reached into my chest and hugged my fucking heart. Were those tears I felt in the corners of my eyes?

I inhaled a sharp breath and whispered back, "I love you too, Kat. I never stopped." I couldn't say any more because I'd fucking cry. I could feel the ball of nerves working up in my throat, so I ended it there instead of telling her I was madly in love with her and had adopted a dog just so she didn't lose it. I didn't say any of that, and damn, how I wish I had.

Instead, I closed my eyes, pulled Kat closer, and slept better than I had in years.

23

KELLY

Something was licking my feet. I knew Greyson and I had some pretty kinky sex when we wanted to, but the man had yet to lick my feet. I was not into feet licking!

"Greyson?" I asked, panicked. *Where is he?*

I sat up, pulling my toes in close, seeing Jet's black head rise above the bed.

"Aww, bud, are you awake and want us to be awake?" I flipped the covers over, wincing at how sore I was when I went to throw my legs over the side. I looked back, hoping maybe Greyson would carry me downstairs or something, anything to avoid walking…but he wasn't in bed.

Feeling my eyebrows dip in confusion, I stood and headed to the bathroom. Peeing hurt. Everything hurt, because I had begged Greyson to ruin me the night before. Just the memory of all we'd done had my core heating and my legs clenching.

I wanted it again. And again, and again.

I never wanted it to end with him. I had never felt more desired or safe than I did with him. Him in control of my arousal, in control of our bodies...there was something so insanely sexy about a man who knew not just how to take control, but how to use it.

After cleaning up in the bathroom and finding a pair of sweats and a t-shirt, I ventured downstairs.

"Greyson?" I called out while descending the stairs. I could smell coffee brewing, which was a good sign.

Jet ran alongside me, eager to be let out. "Here you go, boy." I opened the sliding glass door leading to the back yard.

Greyson was outside on the phone, wearing a black hoodie and a pair of low-slung sweatpants. With his disheveled hair, he looked like a sexy pajama god sent to snuggle and sex me to death.

He waved at me, smiling, but he was caught up in listening to whoever was on the other end of the call, his face pensive and tight. I left him to finish up and headed back inside, searching for the coffee.

I was about to pour myself a cup when someone rang the doorbell. I looked over toward the back door, wondering if Greyson would come back in, but after a few seconds, it was clear he wouldn't be.

One more ring and I was padding toward the front door, swinging it open.

Nothing could have prepared me for seeing Mr. Knox again, the man who had ruined my chances at law school, at interning, at love...all of it had been ripped away from me, and for what?

I didn't say anything, too stunned to even acknowledge that he was standing there.

"What on earth are you doing here?" he asked, his eyes sizing me up, starting at my hair and going down to my feet. His disgust was apparent in how his lip curled, his white eyebrows rising to his hairline, and those eyes—blue, cold, and assessing.

They weighed and measured and then obliterated.

"I'm with Greyson," I replied curtly. I didn't owe him a response, not an explanation or anything close to it.

"I can see that, but why?" he asked, his voice shrill and flustered.

"That's none of your business." I huffed, nearly laughing at his audacity.

His features softened the slightest bit, the rigid line in his shoulders nearly melting as he relaxed.

"That's not how I meant it—it's just that Greyson is a taken man," he said hesitantly, which I hated more than him saying it with passion or fire.

Hesitance implied concern, and I didn't want any concern from this man. Not ever.

"Thank you, but I'm not worried about that," I said, ready to push the door closed.

I wouldn't believe him. Of course, just hearing that ripped my heart into shreds, but it was papier-mâché anyway, ripped and glued back together. Messy, ugly—recycled.

"Look, I have no reason to lie to you, and I didn't know you'd be here. I came to discuss Greyson's engagement plans... there's something Tessa needs to tell him regarding the venue, but she hasn't been able to get through all night." Mr. Knox pleaded with his eyes. They'd turned gentle now, calm as a tranquil sea.

Playing his game, I crossed my arms and asked, "Then why didn't Tessa come here to check, and why wasn't she here last night?"

Mr. Knox furrowed his brows, taking a step back. "She's out of town at the moment. She'll be devastated once she learns about this betrayal."

He shook his head, not watching anymore, and my heart was doing something funny. It was wilting, dying in the sun that had just burst into my life. Greyson had broken up the cloudy skies in my life, and now I was basking in the glow.

"No...I don't believe you, not after what you did." I shook my head, shoving my shoulder into the doorframe.

"I know I messed up a few years back, a short-sighted decision on my end, but trust me when I say I have no ulterior motive for lying to you. I gain nothing."

Fear snaked its way through my chest, threatening to strangle me. I couldn't go through it again; I wouldn't survive.

"You need to leave," I declared, stepping back and slamming the door in his face.

He was wrong—he was lying. There was no way, not after the previous night, after everything he'd done. I wouldn't make the same mistake Greyson had and believe his father, wouldn't let him ruin us. I just needed to shake off the encounter and talk to Grey.

I peeked out the sliding door and saw him still pacing, waving his hands around, staring down. Whoever he was talking to, it seemed serious. I heaved a heavy sigh and decided to start in on that cup of coffee, curling up on the couch while I caught up on my emails.

The problem with having the internet at your fingertips is the danger that comes with unlimited knowledge.

I stayed in my inbox for exactly three solid minutes before my fingers drifted toward the search bar. I hated myself for it, but surely *if* someone was marrying into the Knox family and it was well established, there'd be some news article out there to corroborate the story.

I typed in Tessa James and Greyson Knox, hating how their names looked next to each other. I waited, tapping the news option at the top, and prayed nothing would load, unless it was from four years earlier.

Instead, there was link after link, all under Twitter, in addition to some blog or pop culture site.

Narrowing my gaze, I clicked the first link, dated most recent, and was taken to Twitter.

There, on the screen, was an image of Tessa. She had her ring finger out, a massive diamond resting there—but it wasn't the ring that had my stomach dropping out from underneath me; it was the mirror she was looking into. There was a splash of grey walls and recessed lighting that cast an almost eerie glow over the space.

That was Greyson's downstairs guest bathroom. I looked over my shoulder toward it, a sick, nauseous feeling settling in.

A glutton for punishment, I clicked on the next link. It was an image of Tessa looking in another mirror, and the caption read: *Future wifey of Dr. Knox.*

I was going to be sick.

I could barely breathe. The last photo I clicked on was from about three weeks ago, and it was an image of Tessa and Greyson together while they were in college. I wasn't sure where she'd gotten the photo—it was a throwback for sure— but the time frame had me confused. As far as I knew, Tessa and Greyson had never dated prior to the stunt they pulled… but…was I wrong?

The two were close, Greyson's arm around Tessa, the top of her head tucked under him…the shirt he wore…it was the year we had dated, but when had he ever been that close to her?

The stinging tears running down my face proved that it didn't matter.

He'd done it again—he'd played me, regardless of what he'd told me in bed.

I didn't know what to believe or what to do…except leave, do exactly what I'd done four years earlier: tuck tail and run…run until the pain receded.

24

GREYSON

I SLIPPED BACK into the house, feeling aggravated and hating that the joy I had from the previous night, from finally fixing things with Kat was now overshadowed by some bullshit politics my father was trying to play.

I had called Josh early this morning to fill him in on everything Sienna had told me; it was a mess, and if anyone could help me sort it, it was him. However, he was going through his own shit mess that didn't leave him much margin for time. Still, it was nice to have an ally as I worked to make a plan. I was going to ruin Tessa James and bury her in legal shit, right alongside my father.

The house smelled like coffee, but it was too quiet. Kat's mornings had always been loud when we were together. She said it helped her to wake up; either music or the television would be on while she cooked or got ready...she didn't like a quiet house.

Concerned, I ran upstairs, calling her name. Jet followed behind me, letting out a little whine...she wasn't anywhere.

"What the hell?" I asked, rubbing the back of my neck. The shirt she'd worn was deposited on my bed; her dress and heels that had been in the corner were gone. Why would she leave without saying anything?

Sitting down on the bed, I pulled my cell back out and dialed her. It rang through until I got her voicemail.

"Hey, it's me…just checking on you. I didn't know you had anywhere to go this morning. Sorry about that phone call, it was Josh…call me back."

I hesitated with saying I loved her…I wasn't sure why. It made me feel too vulnerable, especially when deep down, I could feel that something was off. The shit with Tessa was too close to the surface, and Kat hadn't heard my side of anything. At any moment, she could see something and get the wrong impression of what was happening.

"Shit," I muttered to myself, scrubbing a hand down my face.

I jumped in the shower, got dressed, and headed out, hoping to find her.

One week later

"Good morning, Dr. Knox," Payton said, barely loud enough for me to hear. My red, watery eyes tracked her head tilt, but I didn't miss how she glared at me from under her lashes, or how her not getting up spoke a thousand words. Her and every other person in the shelter.

"Morning," I mumbled back, quickly moving to the back. I was hungover again, and again, it wasn't the smartest decision considering I had a surgery in two hours.

I sat down at the makeshift desk they'd set up for me when I originally started and opened my laptop, double-checking all the details about the surgery I had scheduled: chocolate Lab found last night, three masses on his stomach. I checked to see who my assistants would be, and when I saw who was scheduled, I nearly fell out of my chair.

Kat.

She was back? I stood, quickly moving to the door, power-walking down the hall, and pushing through into her office—only to find her desk empty, just like it had been for the past week.

I turned on my heel and shuffled back toward the front. "Payton, is my schedule correct? Is Kat coming in today?" I asked, practically yelling at the poor girl.

Her brows furrowed in confusion. "Who's Kat?"

Right—only I called her that. *Shit.*

I rubbed the back of my neck, wishing the tension would dissipate, while I calmly responded, "Sorry...that's what I call her...ugh. I meant Kelly—is she coming in today to help me with my surgery?"

Payton's face bounced back faster than a rubber band, her cold resolve snapping back into place. "Yes. She is."

That was it. Payton ducked her head and continued working on the pile of paperwork in front of her.

I knew why she was mad. It was the same reason half the camera crew, the rest of the volunteers, and likely every person in Temecula hated me.

Tessa James had gone on national television with her shit story about how the animal doctor playing at love with his director ex-girlfriend was a fraud. She had photos of what looked like me but wasn't. The man in the pictures always had his back to the camera, or his hat on, hiding his face. She did, however, have a few pictures of my house and of my fucking dog.

It was nearly irrefutable evidence that we were together. I knew from what Sienna had told me that my father was behind it all. Payback for abandoning the firm, payback because he hated Kat's family…it was all a massive clusterfuck. Everyone hated me, and Kat hadn't been around for me to talk to her.

She disappeared after that night together. No phone calls, no social media. I checked with Selah and stalked her apartment; she was nowhere, and we never talked about what the hell had happened.

I wasn't an idiot; I knew it revolved around Tessa with the timing of everything, but I had no idea how to fix it.

Now I'd be seeing Kat for the first time in a week and it would be during a surgery…I wasn't even sure my camera crew was still coming in or not. I hadn't talked to them in a few days, not after they'd muttered "Asshole" and "Liar" at me a few times before packing up and leaving.

Just like my re-entry into Kat's life, I knew I had to do something big to get her back, to prove this wasn't a big prank, a lie…all the things she had been worried about four years earlier.

I went back to my office space, downing coffee, water, and pain relievers so I would be ready for surgery. I didn't leave my little area for any reason until it was time to get in that room, because I didn't trust myself not to go to Kat begging on my hands and knees.

Around ten, I headed toward the operating station with fresh gloves and my mask in place, and I tried not to react to seeing Kat already there, ready to go. She had a newer volunteer standing next to her, and the two of them were laughing and joking about something. Neither looked my way when I entered.

It wasn't until Leo, one of our seniors, entered with the dog that Kat's eyes finally swung my way. I wished so badly that I could see more of her face, but her surgical mask covered everything but those beautiful eyes.

Blue-green specks of gold…not vibrant today…they were muted, cold…angry.

"Good morning, Ms. Thomas. It's nice to see you," I started, trying to put my best professional foot forward.

She nodded. "Dr. Knox."

My chest squeezed at how formal and foreign she sounded… but it was something. At least she wasn't ignoring me.

"I appreciate your help with this surgery. We'll get him set up, and we're going to be removing the masses from his stomach."

She kept her eyes fluctuating between the table and my face, not responsive, no emotion.

"Sounds good."

The other two volunteers stayed in the room with us while we worked, making it impossible for the two of us to talk. It was torture, seeing her, smelling her, being this close but so far away. I needed to talk to her, needed to hear what it was she'd seen or heard. I needed to know how I could fix it.

Once we were finished, Kat laughed with the volunteers like everything was fine. She washed up, ignored me, and headed back to work.

That was how our relationship was going to go from here on out. She was freezing me out, a stone-cold wall of professionalism, and there was nothing I could do about it.

I waited outside the shelter like a creep. It had been almost an hour since my shift ended. I could have made up excuses to stay, but knowing Kat, she'd just be the one to leave first, and she'd go when I wasn't looking too. So, I made the first move, to throw her off.

The second the door opened and she shoved through, I was next to her.

"Ride with me?" I asked. It was stupid, but it was also raining.

She stopped, turned on her heel, and stared at me like I was a stranger, someone intent on hurting her. "No thank you, Dr. Knox."

Fuck.

"Kat, please! What happened? Why did you just leave? Where have you been?" I followed her quick pace, pleading with her to answer.

She didn't.

"I called you about a million times, sent you texts, direct messages on social media…I was about to hire a PI just to find you," I continued, sounding pathetic and desperate—because I was. She'd turned me into a raving madman. "Kat, come on!" I begged, pulling on her hand, spinning her toward me.

"No, Greyson, you come on!" she yelled, pushing at my chest. "Your father showed up, wondering why I was at your house. He looked disgusted with me, which he confirmed when he said you were a promised man! He told me you and Tessa James are set to be married this fall and I was the other woman —a fucking idiot," she screamed, holding her hand out in fury.

"Kat, he lied. He has been on this mission to ruin my life ever since I turned him down about the family firm. He knew we were at the benefit together, and he likely assumed we'd be together that morning. He played us." I kept my voice calm, drilling in every point with force. I needed her to hear me.

She shook her head back and forth, blinking while she stepped back. "I saw pictures of her in your house. You are the liar, Greyson. *You*. Leave me alone. Whatever this was, it's over."

She shoved her hands in her pockets and power-walked toward the bus stop, where one had just pulled in.

Shit. This was a mess. Of course she assumed I was the liar— she'd believed it for four years because I'd never fixed what I had broken. I'd never clarified anything for her. For four years, I had let her release her dreams, let her keep her head down and not engage with anyone from our social circles. I'd done this. I'd broken her.

I needed to fix it, fix her, repair this damage once and for all.

25

KELLY

THINGS FELT BRITTLE, unstable, like they were about to break apart any second. The week I spent up at my father's house in Napa was much needed. After everything had happened four years earlier, he'd packed up his practice and moved north, ready to break ties with the toxic Knox family and everyone associated with them.

I would have followed him, and did for a while, but Selah had settled in Temecula with Bryan, and I lived for my sister and those boys. So, I stayed.

My father, a fierce hater of the Knox family, was oddly skeptical of Greyson's part in this whole thing. I'd spilled all the details about how Mr. Knox had shown up, telling me about this supposed relationship with Tessa. I admitted that it did sound fishy, and without the proof from Tessa's Twitter feed, I wouldn't have believed him. But, there were pictures, and that was enough to prove Greyson had lied.

She had been in his house, his *new* house.

While I was soaking in the sun in Napa, tending to my broken heart, I saw the interview with Tessa on some morning show. Picture after picture, including one with Jet that nearly eviscerated whatever was left of my heart. She accused Greyson of using me to build followers, accused him of cheating and who knows what else. My father turned the television off and promised I didn't need to hear the rest.

Maybe I didn't.

In the end, it didn't matter. Greyson had been with Sienna all night then I'd thrown myself at him, demanding he fuck me before explaining it all to me. Honestly, I'd assumed he would tell the horrible truth about him moving on to Tessa, choosing her over me. I'd wanted to be numb to it, wanted some other kind of pain to feel in my body, something other than heartbreak.

That's why I demanded he be rough with me, because I trusted Greyson with my body, completely...it was just my heart I wasn't so sure about.

One week away wasn't enough time to get him out of my system or to heal the heartbreak, but it was enough time to stand firm about my feelings and not crumble the first time he spoke to me. It also gave me time to think over a proposition from my father.

"Come, live here with me. Go to law school, take the bar exam...come be a part of the family company." I toyed with the offer all week, every night. It gave me something to think about other than Greyson.

I could come back and visit on the weekends...or at least some weekends. Napa was about an eight-hour drive from Temecula, but I could fly. I could see Selah plenty, and there was video chat.

I'd always wanted to be a lawyer, but whenever I considered leaving the animal shelter, there was this tiny sliver of remorse that snuck in. That was enough to make me doubt leaving, because it was no longer just about Selah, or the boys. It was also about this new life I'd carved out for myself and these animals. It was about doing something that mattered.

Heartbreak aside, I wanted to keep doing something that mattered.

I was just getting back from the grocery store, a few bags in my arms, when I saw a crumpled form sitting against my door.

Greyson.

Trying to act confident, I walked up, set my bags down, and pulled my keys free.

Greyson stood, his eyes watery, contrasting with the flowers in his hand, which were brilliant and bold, beautiful.

"Hey," I muttered, wishing my heart wasn't beating as hard as it was. He'd brought me flowers!

"Hey," he said somberly, leaning down to pick up a grocery bag. I didn't want him in my space. I didn't want him near me, but I wasn't about to have a big fight out in my hall.

I pushed the door open, Greyson following behind with the rest of the groceries.

I set mine down then began pulling all the items free.

"Kat, I need to tell you what I wanted to say that night… before we…" He trailed off.

"Before we fucked?" I asked, confident and brazen. I didn't want to be broken while I was around him, not where he could see anyway.

"Yeah...if you remember, there was something I wanted to tell you." He rubbed the back of his neck. His light jacket covered a simple white V-neck t-shirt, and his jeans were designer, perfectly tailored for his strong legs and tall frame. I hated how handsome he was.

I turned away from the counter, crossing my arms. "Was it that you're engaged?"

He scoffed, shaking his head. "No...fuck." He exhaled and grabbed his hair.

I waited, knowing already, somewhere deep down, that he was telling the truth. That revelation unsettled me, but I wouldn't show it. Not yet. I needed to think about it a little bit more first.

"That night at the benefit, I was standing with Sienna for a large chunk of the night." His blue eyes watched me, waiting.

How could I forget that little barb of hurt?

Suddenly, I wasn't sure I could handle what he was about to say next, but I didn't want him to know that. I clenched my arms in a death lock, waiting for him to deliver his story.

"Well, Sienna is someone I've known almost my whole life— our families go way back. Anyway, the reason I was standing next to her all night is that she mentioned overhearing a juicy piece of gossip that might interest me. It had to do with Tessa James."

My heart pitter-pattered under my shirt, curious where he was going with this. This wasn't what I was expecting at all.

"Josh was the first person to find these weird tweets from Tessa about still being with me. He warned me about it a few weeks ago, but I didn't want to say anything because it was such a touchy subject with us. I was sure you'd just write me off and believe her over me the first second you saw it."

Ouch. That was exactly what I *had* done.

"So, I was trying to gather what info I could on what her angle was. She started posting right around the time you and I became YouTube famous and that show ran our video." He paused, waiting for me to respond, but now I was too invested to interrupt.

This felt right, felt true, and in my gut, I knew he wasn't lying.

"So, Josh started digging into it. Meanwhile, you and I started spending more time together and connecting, which was my entire goal in coming here, so I didn't pay any attention to what was brewing behind the scenes." He stepped closer, still watching me with those heavy blue eyes. "Sienna told me she was walking in the hall outside my father's office a few days before the benefit...she saw Tessa in the office, and knowing what Tessa had been claiming on social media, she waited outside the door. She heard them talking about a contract and a payout. She heard my father say that as soon as you were out of the picture once and for all, he'd deposit the money."

What the hell? My stomach dropped, suddenly famished and weary from all the little bits of food I'd managed to get down, none of it enough for any proper nutrition. I needed to sit. Closing my eyes tight, I turned around and started vigorously putting away all the perishables from my grocery run.

"I'm launching an investigation into it. I'm suing Tessa for all the false claims she made about me and for breaking and entering into my house. Notice the pictures she has of me never show my face?" Greyson stepped around me, standing close enough to touch me. Some deep part of me wanted him to...needed him to.

"Except that one from when we were in college," I muttered.

His eyes searched mine, then fell. "Yeah...that one was real. Nothing ever happened between us, but I never stopped how flirtatious she was with me. It's how I knew she'd be the perfect person to pretend be engaged to back then." He stepped even closer.

My heart thrashed violently, like it'd been tossed into turbulent waters. My brain said to walk away—Greyson had hurt me before, he'd hurt me again—but my heart said he cared. He loved me, he cherished me.

"Greyson...I need—"

He gripped my waist, cutting me off with his lips at my ear. "Time? Space?" he asked, low and desperate. "Take whatever you need, but Kat, come back to me. You've been it for me since we dated in college. I wanted to marry you then. I plan to marry you at some point now. I want only you, forever. I'm *in* love with you, Kat."

Tears burned the corners of my eyes, my lungs straining as if I'd just completed a marathon with no training. He was so close and making this so hard.

"Just give me a..." His lips crashed against mine, hungry and full of wrath.

He pulled me into him, pressing his firm hand against my spine, holding me still while he moved his lips against mine. Tired of fighting it, I let go and wrapped my arms around his neck, pulling him closer to me.

This was what I'd wanted all those years. I'd wanted him to find me, break through my walls, and heal me.

Our bodies molded to one another, heated and desperate. His kiss was savage, tugging and pulling and searing all along my jaw and down my neck.

"I can't lose you again," he whispered into my skin, like he was swearing an oath, speaking into my very veins. "I *won't* lose you again."

He lifted me up, set me on the counter, and tugged my shirt up until it was discarded and on the floor. His strokes against my tongue were desperate and hot, a kiss that burned and cooled, broke and healed. We split apart for only a second before his lips were back against mine, promising me, swearing to me.

His hands moved to my bra, cupping me through the thin fabric, kneading my sensitive buds into hard, painful nubs. I released a moan against his lips, tugging at the hair at the back of his head.

He disconnected from me, stepping back, staring at me with such raw emotion that I nearly broke from the intensity. He moved a few pieces of my hair to the side before tracing my lip with his thumb.

A second later he grabbed me, like I was his bride and he was about to run away with me. He carried me all the way down the hall to my room, where he laid me out on my bed.

He stood above me, just staring again. It made this warm sensation fill my chest, like he was watching in awe or some kind of wonder; it made me feel cherished.

"I'm so in love with you," he whispered, before leaning down to flick the button on my jeans. Slowly, he peeled them down my legs, kissing my thighs while he went. Once both my feet were free, he held my ankle up and ran his finger down the back of my leg then along the outside of my cotton thong.

"Greyson." I sighed, loving his touch.

He repeated the process with the other finger, along the other leg, until he was swiping up and down along my underwear, right over my slit. He smiled, gently pushing against the fabric, until he bunched the middle of the material together and pulled it tight against my entrance.

"Look how soaked you're getting it," he rumbled, moving the material up and down my slit, the backs of his fingers just barely touching my opening.

It was insanely erotic, my hips rotating upward of their own accord, chasing the promise of friction.

Finally, he let me go, stood, and removed his clothing, until he was naked in front of me. Smiling and staring down at me, he stroked himself. Meanwhile, I still wore my sports bra and my soaked underwear.

"Touch yourself," he rasped while watching me.

Obeying him, I slid my hand down to my stomach, about to dip under the elastic of my thong, but he stopped me.

"Over it, like I did," he instructed.

Licking my lips, I did as he said, rubbing my fingers over the wet material at my core. My other hand went to my breast, massaging it through my bra, loving the look of lust in his eyes.

"Now bunch it together and move it up and down like I did." He licked his lips, stroking his hard cock up and down.

I did as he said, gathering the fabric like he had, rubbing the backs of my fingers along my middle.

"Pull harder—let me see how wet you're getting," he demanded.

I did as he said, pulling on the cotton, a moan escaping from me in the process.

Feeling bold and needy, I moved the scrap of fabric to the side, baring myself to him.

"Tell me how wet I am for you."

His eyes blazed with lust, a sound of pleasure winding up from his sternum. "So wet."

He pulled my legs forward until I was close to the edge of the bed. His dick was poking at my entrance, at my covered pussy. Rubbing his shaft along my slit, he pushed the material farther into my core, stretching it and soaking it as he drove into me.

"Greyson," I cried desperately.

He kept nudging his cock in and out, rubbing, dry-humping me—except the thin material was shoved to the side from the friction, so I was getting more and more soaked by the second, relishing the velvet feel of his rigid shaft.

Falling forward, he caged me in with his strong arms while he moved us back on the bed, all the while continuing his assault against my core.

"Greyson, I can't…" I breathed out, barely containing my lust.

"You need more, baby?" he prodded, taking my nipple into his mouth.

"Yes!" I bucked my hips, desperate to find a way to get his dick inside me.

He was so close.

Thankfully, he dipped his hand between us and shoved the material to the side until it was tightly pinned against the side of my hips.

He thrust into me, causing my breath to catch.

"Yesssss," I moaned, clutching his shoulders.

His hips lifted as he pushed down into my center. His hand went around me, down to my ass, squeezing it tight while he moved in me.

Our breaths mingled, my covered breasts pushing against his firm chest, the hardened nipples pressing through the thin material. I loved it like this.

His lips crashed against mine while he increased his rhythm.

Long strokes, hot sensual breaths mixing between us as we both became unraveled, each of us chasing our own release, sealing this decision between us. He was mine now, and I wasn't letting him go.

Later that night, after I'd packed a bag and gone to his house, we were tucked under the covers, tracing each other's hands in the dark, and I decided to confess.

"I should tell you…I have a date planned with another man."

Silence met me as I waited for him to respond. Finally, after a few moments of his gentle strokes on my skin, he replied.

"That so?" He ran his fingers down my rib cage and back up.

"Yeah, set for tomorrow night." I resisted the urge to laugh, because we both knew I wasn't keeping it anymore, but it was fun pretending with him.

"Guess I'll just have to ruin you again," he joked, reaching for my breast.

I smiled in the dark, loving his response.

"Guess so," I murmured, hoping he'd make good on his promise.

His mouth descended to my lips a moment later, his body moving over mine.

He lifted himself, bracketing me with his arms while he promised, "You're mine, Kat, and I'm never letting you go. Not for anyone, or anything. Understand?" He leaned down to kiss my neck.

I smiled, moving my hand up his back. "Understood."

"I love you," he whispered against my lips before gently pressing a kiss there.

I held his jaw in my hand, leaning forward. So soft and gentle, I pressed my lips to his.

"I love you too. I'm sorry I believed your dad, and I'm sorry I doubted you. From now on, I'll carry you in my heart so I'll never have to lose you again."

Greyson held me so tight I thought I might crack, but I didn't mind cracking for him, with him—as long as we did it together.

The next day, Greyson and I arrived together.

The shelter was already in full swing as we'd decided to get in a bit later. Holding hands, I relished the look on Payton's face as she zeroed in on the contact then sputtered her latte out.

I appreciated that everyone had seemingly taken my side, but now I needed them to see that I stood with Greyson.

Fierce and protective at my back, Greyson walked me to my office.

"There's something I need to go take care of." He pressed a soft kiss to my hairline.

On instinct, I wondered what it was, not really a jealousy, but a curiosity, a desire to protect him and know how to prepare.

"Can I know what it is?" I asked, laying a hand on his chest.

"It'll be better when you see." He kissed my knuckles, gave me one last smile, and sauntered out.

Of course, there were still parts of me that worried about the other shoe dropping, worried about being pranked and humiliated, but I held tight to the belief that Greyson wouldn't hurt me, not ever again.

The second I plopped down into my chair, I received a FaceTime request from Aubrey. Raising the phone, I slid the accept button over.

"Hey Aubrey." I smiled.

Her lips were thinned, worry etched into her features. "Hey girl, I just wanted to check in with you. We haven't really talked since you told me about taking a quick trip to Napa...I mean, it didn't take a genius to know it had something to do with the gossip train running amok."

She leaned forward, and the shifting revealed Chance's arm. It made me smile, especially knowing Chance had created something of a friendship with Greyson.

They were both worried about us...and probably the shelter.

"Sorry about that. Honestly, it's just one big fat mess. Greyson's dad is a monster, and he orchestrated this whole publicity stunt to get us to break up and try to force Greyson back to his father's firm."

"Christ!" Chance muttered in the background with his thick accent.

"Yeah, crazy stuff," I muttered.

"Wait...break up? That means you two were together?" Aubrey asked excitedly.

I blushed, ducking my head. "For literally less than twenty-four hours before all the shit hit the fan."

"Aww, no fair. Well how about now?" she asked, leaning back. I could see her round belly and smiled.

"You're getting so big!" I said on instinct.

Aubrey smiled, lowering her gaze to her midsection. "Oh my god, right?!" She laughed, rubbing it. That white furry head bleated behind them, trying to shove its face into her lap. "Pixy is already so jealous of his little brother." She rolled her eyes.

"You have to do a photo shoot with them both, you do realize that, right?" I joked, smiling at the screen, picturing a hilarious shoot with Pixy and baby Chance.

"We already have a photographer booked, but by then we'll be back in LA. You and Greyson will have to come and see us!" she declared. "Wait, did we establish that you're back together or not?" She tilted her head.

I laughed. "We are...officially back together."

"Yay!" She clapped her hands excitedly.

"Well, I have to go," I said, eyeing the clock, knowing I had an appointment with a donor in less than fifteen minutes.

"Okay, bye! Keep us posted!" Aubrey said hopefully before disconnecting the call.

I couldn't wait to see her again and have her living close again. It had been way too long since we'd had a cup of coffee together.

The rest of the day flew by, all of it without seeing Greyson. I started to worry around the end of my shift, especially when one of his surgeries had to be rescheduled.

It wasn't until Payton ran into my office screaming that I had some idea of what was going on.

"Turn on your television!"

She came to a stop in my room, but I didn't have a television in my office. She pushed me aside from my desk with her bony shoulder and started vigorously typing on my laptop.

"What are you—" I asked, leaning back.

"Shhhh, just look!" she yelled.

Another volunteer ran into my office, breathing hard, eyes wide.

Before I could ask what on earth was happening, the screen loaded: a local television station was broadcasting a YouTube clip with the news reporter's commentary on how it had been sent in to their station.

The clip was of Greyson sitting in a chair, talking to the camera.

"Hello, I'm Greyson Knox. Many of you saw a woman named Tessa James claim to be my fiancée on a few morning shows and likely saw it spread all over social media. I'm here to set the record straight." He leaned forward, making an arch with his fingers.

My heart flipflopped in my chest as he continued.

"My father is a ruthless attorney and owns one of the largest firms in the state. He's less than ethical and needed more shares in the firm as one of the partners was retiring. His hopes were for me to join, buy those shares, and then essentially own more than his partners. He'd have full control of what was done, and what wasn't. He has helped more than a few dirty politicians, cops, corporations—you name it, they've bought him. Because of this, he felt the need to force me into working with him." He paused, ducking and shaking his head. "I chose to become a veterinarian instead, something where I could help heal animals—something far away from my father's footsteps. He's been trying to find a way to force my hand since I started at the Park Avenue Animal Shelter. So, he hired Tessa James to stage that we were in a relationship. Why?"

My stomach clenched tight as Payton and the other girl huddled closer to me.

"Because the world saw that I was in love with Kelly Thomas, director of the shelter. My camera crew caught moments between us, and I guess everyone saw what I was wearing so obviously on my face and in my actions. The world was calling us America's sweethearts, we were instantly famous, and my father saw a golden opportunity to strike.

"I haven't ever been in any kind of relationship with Tessa James, and she is now and has always been an easy hire for dirty work. She broke into my apartment to obtain photos of my house and pet. The photos she used that were supposed to be of me were of a paid actor or friend. Notice my face isn't shown in any of those images, other than one from when we were friends back in college.

"I'd like to set the record straight. So…" He scooted his chair back, the camera guys shifting to give him space.

He knelt down on one knee.

Oh my god.

"Kelly Arabella Thomas, Kat…I know I've messed up, missed the opportunities you gave me, and almost lost you forever more times than I care to count, but I love you. You are my life, my whole world. I need you by my side as I walk out the rest of this life. Will you make me the happiest man in the world and marry me?"

He opened a velvet box with a diamond ring tucked inside.

I was numb. Surely this was a dream. Had he actually just proposed to me on national television?

Someone was shaking my shoulders, and I turned to see Payton smiling at me.

"Kel, oh my gosh!" She jumped up and down.

Tears welled in my eyes as I blinked, looking around the room. *Where is he? How long ago was that?*

I scooted back, desperate to find him.

Running out of my office, I spun around the corner, coming to a quick stop.

There on the floor in the middle of the shelter, Jet by his side, the camera crew lined up along the wall, was Greyson. He held that black box and that smile I knew was only for me.

My heart rioted inside my chest, telling me, *Go, go, go!*

I walked toward him, slowly, wiping at my eyes. They were traitorous.

"Kat, baby…" he whispered.

A sob worked its way up my throat as I closed the distance between us. At the last second, he stood, and I threw myself at him.

"I love you—yes! A million times yes," I said into his ear.

He hugged me tight, his voice tight with emotion just like mine. "I love you, baby. I love you so much." He lowered me then slammed his lips to mine.

We didn't care that we were being filmed, or that our volunteers were watching, or that Julie had Chance and Aubrey pulled up on a laptop screen watching on, Aubrey blubbering with a Kleenex in her hand.

I kissed him passionately, claiming this man, this vicious vet as my own, once and for all.

The End

EPILOGUE

SIX MONTHS LATER

I STOOD STARING at the one thing that might ruin my relationship with my fiancé. White skin with a pinkish hue, equally fair hair cascading along her back, blue eyes...brown spots, and a wide, pink snout.

"She can't come in here." I crossed my arms in defiance.

Greyson looked up from where he knelt next to her. "But she's cold."

I looked up at the sky for help and confirmation that it was still the middle of summer. I knew it was summer, because it was hot, but also because I had been counting down the days until Greyson went back to school. He was going to be close to home for on-campus classes, along with doing a mix of online courses to complete his undergrad schooling.

We were in the process of hiring a new vet for the shelter, a bittersweet feeling, but we couldn't have a new baby while he did school full-time *and* have him volunteer at the shelter. He said he would do it and it would be fine, but it was me who drew the line there and refused him.

"It's almost one hundred and ten degrees outside—pretty sure she's fine."

"Fine then, she's hot." He stood, putting his hands on his hips.

This was the fifth random animal he'd brought home to our ranch-style house just outside the city limits of Temecula. It was a four-bedroom home, which we planned to fill with children—and, apparently, animals. Jet lifted his head from inside the screened porch, not at all surprised by this turn of events.

"Baby, please." Greyson pouted his lips, bringing his hands up in a praying motion.

"I'm so glad you brought him up." I stepped closer, pressing a finger into his chest. "I am having a baby in just five months, and I don't want a pig running around our house while we're first-time parents."

"But babe, by then, she'll be adopted, and it'll be fine." He shifted closer, putting his arms around me, bringing my body flush with his chest.

"That's what you said about Henry."

I could feel the laughter bubble up from inside him. "Does our little hedgehog really bother you that much?"

I turned, facing him, while he kept me caged against his body. "Of course not. I love Henry, but we don't have the best track record of finding these animals homes. Besides, doesn't it look bad on me as the director of an animal shelter that I can't find adoptive homes for these pets?" I waved a hand toward the pig at our feet, who was sniffing the air.

"These aren't exactly cats and dogs—it's not easy to find adoptive parents for a pig, or a hedgehog, or a horse."

My eyes went wide. "Since when are we calling Jack a horse?"

"He is a horse!" Greyson argued.

"He's barely three feet tall!"

The soon-to-be father of my child and my future husband gasped in shock at my comment.

"That is so rude I don't even know what to say to you right now. What if he heard you?" Greyson bent back down to pay attention to the pig.

I let out a sigh. "The barn is behind our house, for one, and two, he's deaf. You know that, I know that…we all know that."

"He's just stubborn," Greyson countered.

I knew I wasn't getting anywhere with this, and I had to pee.

"Fine. Five months—that's it!"

"That's it, we promise." Greyson stood, pulling me into a kiss.

I smiled against his mouth, because for all my talk, I loved that he had such a big heart. I loved that he was such a softie when it came to these animals.

"Don't forget that Chance, Aubrey, the baby, and Pixy are coming to stay with us for the weekend," I said, moving into the house.

"Pixy is going to love what I did to the goat area of the barn." Greyson rubbed his hands together.

I laughed, tossing my head back. This man.

"Grey, you do realize Pixy is like their child, right? He'll sleep in the same room as them…probably, maybe. We should make sure Jack is ready, though." I could see the wheels already turning in his head. "No. No way," I said, stomping toward the kitchen.

243

"If they can have an indoor pet and be parents, why can't we?" he yelled at my retreating back.

"No indoor pigs!" I yelled back, smiling, cherishing this life I led, this full and amazing life.

I stopped to remember what things had been like six months prior when Greyson had proposed on television. It had gone viral, as had my answer to him. It'd played on all the daily talk shows, making the hosts emotional and teary-eyed. We'd received multiple requests to appear on the shows, but we'd turned them all down. If people wanted to see us, they had to watch our YouTube channel, which was still going strong, except we'd let the camera guys go and decided to film it ourselves.

The world got a glimpse of shelter life, our adoptions, and, every now and then, our ranch.

Greyson's father had been investigated after the clip aired, and he was now serving twelve years in prison for a multitude of things, mainly evidence tampering and interfering with a few federal cases. He was still fighting the sentencing, but we were free of him and his web of lies.

Now it was just us, our friends, and these animals.

Perfection I could never have planned for.

Want to keep up with all of the new releases in Vi Keeland and Penelope Ward's Cocky Hero Club world? Make sure you sign up for the official Cocky Hero Club newsletter for all the latest on our upcoming books:

https://www.subscribepage.com/CockyHeroClub

Check out other books in the Cocky Hero Club series:
http://ww.cockyheroclub.com

ALSO BY ASHLEY MUNOZ

All Available to read through Kindle Unlimited

Interconnected Series:

Glimmer

Fade

Standalone's

What Are the Chances

The Rest of Me

Tennessee Truths

ABOUT THE AUTHOR

Ashley resides in the Pacific Northwest, where she lives with her four children and Mr. Fix-It husband. She spends her time trying to convince her kids that the Backstreet Boys are the best band to ever grace the earth, writing fantasy that she'll probably never publish and snuggling her husband while she reads her kindle.

ACKNOWLEDGMENTS

I signed on to write in the Cocky World back in 2019 before the world imploded and everything as we knew it ended. I had started strong with the idea of Kelly and Greyson, but I had time to write it all out, so I took it and relished in the freedom the flexible time schedule provided. Then COVID hit, people died, my kids came home, my husband's job fired over ten thousand people, and everything changed.

I couldn't have written this book without the support of my husband. While we were settling into a new home, shuffling our new normal and dealing with scary headlines - he was there, smiling at me, telling me to write. To finish, to complete this book and to honor my characters story. It seems silly because it's just a book, but to an author: these books, these stories that we tell, are so much more. These characters live inside us, they breathe the same air as us, they keep us up at night and won't leave us alone. I'd also like to thank Tiffany Hernandez, my PA, usual proofreader and good friend. Thank you so much for standing there when I had to remove service after service because my funds were dwindling due to my husband's job reducing hours and furloughing people. Thank you for pushing this story and for helping me to get the notice it deserves.

Thank you to all the other Cocky Authors- your support and friendship means the world to me. Thank you Brittany Taylor and Amy Elizabeth for beta reading this and giving me the courage I needed to keep going and Amy, as always, for catching some of my obvious blunders that would have been really embarrassing if I hadn't caught them.

And to Vi Keeland and Penelope Ward: thank you for opening your world to us. Thank you for taking a chance on us and for allowing us this great pleasure of creating something new within such a wonderful space that didn't really need us at all- I'm so honored to be apart of it.

Printed in Great Britain
by Amazon

74414153R00151